DESERT COMBAT

Book Three in the Secret Squadron Series

GW00708304

One

Tobruk. Before the war it had been a name on the map, a dot on the coastline of North Africa, and nothing more. Now, in the summer of 1941, it was a port of massive importance to those who fought in the blistering desert of Cyrenaica, the only safe and accessible harbour for over a thousand miles, between Sfax in Tunisia and Alexandria in Egypt.

Perhaps 4,000 people had lived in Tobruk in the days before the War, existing in a few hundred buildings that stood out starkly against the sun-baked, rocky ground that sloped down towards a small quay. Their daily bread was earned in handling the goods that were funnelled via Tobruk to the outside world from the vast African hinterland, their thirst quenched by a water distillation plant that produced 40,000 gallons a day. The square in the centre of Tobruk boasted a few dusty palm trees, the only splash of green in the overall drabness of the place.

It was only a few months since Tobruk had been an Italian possession, and the Italians had been conscious of the place's strategic value, for they had built two lines of strong points around it, completely sunk into the ground. The lines covered a forty-mile perimeter at a radius of twenty miles from the town. The outer defences consisted of a series of heavily concreted dugouts, many cleverly improvised from natural caves, each holding up to forty men; they were interconnected by trenches which had pits every few hundred yards for mortars, machine-guns or anti-tank guns. The trenches were roofed in with thin boarding and covered lightly with sand so that they were invisible from even a few yards away. In front of the outer defences there was a belt of barbed wire, up to thirty yards wide in places, and in front of that there was an anti-tank ditch, adapted to follow the lines of ravines wherever possible. Straight-sided, averaging seven feet deep by ten feet wide, the ditch was designed to thwart any attempted crossing by a tracked vehicle.

The inner defence line was constructed to the same pattern, but without the anti-tank ditch. It lay 2,000–3,000 yards behind the outer fortification.

Six months earlier, the harbour of Tobruk had been crammed with Italian ships, bringing supplies for the great army which, under Marshal Rodolfo Graziani, had assembled in a series of fortified camps stretching fifteen miles inland from the coast near Sidi Barani, ready to thrust into Egypt and raise the flag of Benito Mussolini's Fascist Italy over Cairo. All that had stood in Graziani's path, outnumbered ten to one, had been the puny and ill-equipped British Western Desert Force under General Richard O'Connor, a small and energetic Irishman whose chief weapon was his flair for unorthodox tactics.

O'Connor's tiny force had dug in at Mersa Matruh,

a place where Antony and Cleopatra had once relaxed in the inviting sea that lapped against a spotless white beach, and prepared grimly to stop the Italians, or die in the attempt. But Graziani, preoccupied with building up strong supply lines, had never come; and O'Connor, weighing the odds and deciding that his 36,000 men were a match for Graziani's 300,000, had boldly decided to take the initiative. In December 1940, with the 4th Indian Division and the 7th Armoured Division, he had penetrated the Italian lines and taken the enemy completely by surprise, smashing Graziani's forces and chasing them into Libya in a two-day battle that effectively ended the immediate threat to Egypt.

In those dark winter days of 1940, the news of O'Connor's victory had come like a shot in the arm to the hard-pressed British people, reeling under the almost nightly hammer-blows of Hitler's *Luftwaffe* and facing the dark menace of his seemingly invincible army across the Channel. O'Connor had given them what they wanted, and more. By all the rules his outnumbered forces should have halted after giving the enemy a bloody nose; but in January 1941 the redoubtable general, his Western Desert Force now renamed XIII Corps and reinforced by the 6th Australian Division, pressed on to attack the Italian stronghold of Bardia and captured it in a single day, taking 40,000 prisoners. Less than three weeks later the British were in Tobruk, the next port and fortress along the coast, and another 25,000 Italians were in the bag.

There seemed to be no stopping XIII Corps. In front of O'Connor now lay the Jebel Akhdar, the fertile cresent of hills rolling down to the coastline of Cyrenaica, and beyond it the town of Benghazi. Along the coast road, which wound between the Jebel Akhdar and the sea to the Gulf of Sirte, the broken remnants of Graziani's Tenth Army were struggling to escape into Tripolitania.

It was now that O'Connor took his greatest gamble. Although his tanks and trucks were almost falling apart, he hurled them across the appalling, uncharted desert tracks south of Jebel Akhdar in a bid to reach the coast road ahead of the enemy and bar his retreat. On 5 February, the British spearhead made it with half an hour to spare. For the next two days, a fierce battle raged around Beda Fomm as the Italians tried desperately to break through. They failed, and when the two days were ended O'Connor had achieved complete victory. The Italian Tenth Army had been utterly destroyed, and in ten weeks the British had taken 130,000 prisoners, 400 tanks, 1,290 guns and 1,000 trucks – the latter a real windfall, for it had enabled the advance to maintain its momentum.

For a brief time, after the capture of Benghazi, it had seemed that O'Connor might continue his advance into Tripolitania and drive the Italians completely out of North Africa. It would have been a golden opportunity, but it was denied by events on the other side of the Mediterranean. The previous November, the Italians had advanced into Greece from their bases in Albania; the Greeks hammered them in eleven days and pushed them back over the frontier. Four months later the Italians were still making no headway, although they outnumbered the Greeks by two to one. But German forces were massing in Bulgaria, along Greece's northern frontier, and the Greeks had asked for six British divisions to meet an expected German invasion. Those divisions could come from only one place, and that was North Africa; so O'Connor's plans for further conquest had been stifled.

At the end of March 1941 Alexandria and Port Said had been crammed with troops: 60,000 of them, Australian and New Zealand infantry and British gunners, with supporting technical and mechanised units, all awaiting embarkation. The soldiers had been in a cheerful mood, laughing and joking and eager for a change from the endless desert. There was something romantic about fighting on Greek soil; the Allies had fought bitterly there in the previous war and had held the line successfully, and there seemed no good reason why they should not do so again. There had been no pretence of secrecy; everyone, including the Arabs, had gossiped about the expeditionary force and its destination. Some, on a high note of optimism, had even talked of a thrust through southern Europe to attack Germany in the rear.

Meanwhile, an expeditionary force of a different kind had been assembling in Tripolitania, and on a sunny day in March its commander ordered a great parade to be held in Tripoli. The town's Italian colonial population watched, wide-eyed, as a long column of *Panzers* clattered past, their engines roaring, their tracks making a fearful noise on the macadamised streets. In their open turrets the tank commanders stood smartly to attention.

Not far from the saluting base the tanks turned into a side-street and disappeared. The rumbling, clattering column seemed to be never-ending as tank after tank passed in front of the crowd.

On the saluting dais, the expeditionary force's commander was well satisfied with the parade. Only he and the tank commanders knew what was really happening – that each tank, having driven around the block, had actually passed the saluting base four times. Instead of the 400 tanks counted by the spectators, they had actually seen only one hundred.

So far, these were all the tanks at the disposal of the German expeditionary force. And with these, its commander intended not only to retake Cyrenaica, but also spear on to Egypt, and the Suez Canal. First, in order to secure his seaward flank and to provide a supply base for his forces, he would capture the port of Tobruk.

He was confident that he could do it, and his men were confident too. For this was the man who had commanded the 7th *Panzer* Division in France during the dash to the Channel coast in May 1940, nicknamed the 'Ghost Division' because of its reputation for making unexpected appearances not only in front of but also behind the French lines during that brief but spectacular *Blitzkrieg*. His name was Erwin Rommel.

Two

A rmstrong had risen early that morning, as he usually did when an important day lay ahead. His first task, after the usual wash, shave and call of nature, had been to make the laborious climb to *Ark Royal*'s flight deck to supervise the stowage of his personal belongings in his aircraft. Each pilot was allowed ten pounds of kit, which covered the bare essentials but no more.

A refreshing wind was blowing over the aircraft carrier's flight deck. It seemed to be coming from the east, but Armstrong knew from the latest forecast that it would be westerly at higher altitude, which was good, for the fighters would have the benefit of a tailwind. Four hundred miles over water, into a headwind and with only a single engine to sustain you, was a hell of a long way as you watched the needles of your fuel gauges slowly sinking towards the danger mark.

From his vantage point near the stern, bracing himself against the motion of the ship and feeling the throb of the carrier's three powerful turbines against the soles of his shoes, Armstrong looked along the flight deck and thought how small it looked, even though he knew it was 800 feet long. The *Ark Royal* had a maximum complement of seventy-two aircraft but her usual complement was sixty, her Air Group comprising two squadrons of Fairey Swordfish torpedo-bombers and two of Fairey Fulmar fighters.

One of the Swordfish squadrons had been disembarked at Gibraltar to make room for the twenty-four Hawker Hurricanes that were packed tightly together at the rear of the flight deck. In a few hours' time, if all went to plan, they would be landing on the island of Malta, under siege ever since Italy entered the War on Germany's side in June 1940.

The strategically placed island, only seventy miles from Sicily, was the key to British control of the Mediterranean, and therefore the Middle East. On 10 June 1940, the day Italy declared War on the Allies, the island's air defences comprised only five Fairey Swordfish of the Fleet Air Arm, used mainly for anti-aircraft co-operation, and three Gloster Sea Gladiators, hastily assembled from crated components, with a fourth held in reserve.

The Italians carried out seven major air raids on Malta in the first ten days of the War and the Sea Gladiators – immortalised in the popular Press by the names *Faith, Hope* and *Charity* – scored their first success on 22 June, when Sqn Ldr Gordon Burges shot down a lone S.79 reconnaissance aircraft. The Gladiators destroyed two more enemy aircraft in the following week, and on 28 June, by which time only two of the biplanes were still airworthy, four Hawker Hurricanes were flown in from North Africa. Twelve more reinforcement Hurricanes were flown to the island from the carrier *Argus* on 4 August under cover of diversionary operations by Force H, the Royal Navy's Western Mediterranean Task Force, and a complete Hurricane squadron, No 261, was soon operational. In addition, a small striking force gradually built up on the Maltese airfields; this consisted of the Swordfish of No 830 Squadron, Fleet Air Arm, detachments of Wellington bombers from RAF squadrons in the Canal Zone, and detachments of two Sunderland squadrons, Nos 228 and 230. A similar operation by the *Argus* in mid-November, however, was less successful; twelve Hurricanes and two Skuas were flown off, but they encountered strong unforecast headwinds and only four Hurricanes and one Skua reached Malta.

Although Malta was kept supplied in late 1940 by convoys from Alexandria, heavily escorted by the Mediterranean Fleet, providing adequate fighter reinforcements presented an ongoing problem, as these had to make the long and dangerous passage from Gibraltar. On 10 January 1941, newly-arrived *Luftwaffe* dive-bombers based on Sicily joined with the *Regia Aeronautica* to inflict substantial damage on a Malta-bound convoy, including the aircraft carrier *Illustrious*, and after that no further supplies reached the island – which was under almost continual air attack – until the last week in March, when a small convoy of four ships was sent through from Alexandria. Even then, two of the ships and their precious stores were damaged by bombs while unloading.

On 2 April, in an operation codenamed *Winch*, the carrier *Ark Royal*, with a strong Force H escort, set out from Gibraltar carrying twelve Hurricanes and three

Blackburn Skuas; these were flown off at a distance of 400 nautical miles from Malta, and all arrived safely. On 28 April twenty more Hurricanes, ferried from the UK by the *Argus* and transferred to the *Ark Royal* at Gibraltar, were also flown off to Malta, together with three Fulmars, in operation *Dunlop*.

The scene now briefly shifted to Egypt, where the Eighth Army, under heavy pressure from General Erwin Rommel's *Panzerarmee Afrika*, was in urgent need of reinforcements, with particular regard to tanks and fighter aircraft. Between 5 and 12 May 1941, therefore, Force H and the Mediterranean Fleet mounted a joint operation, code-named *Tiger*, to push a convoy of five fast merchantmen carrying the necessary equipment through the Mediterranean from Gibraltar to Alexandria. At the same time, the battleship *Queen Elizabeth* and two light cruisers from UK waters were being sent out to join Admiral Cunningham's fleet. The convoy passed Gibraltar on 6 May and was escorted by Force H to a point south of Malta, where it was covered by destroyers and cruisers from the island base until it could be met by a strong force sent out from Alexandria. Several German and Italian air attacks en route were broken up by Fulmars from the *Ark Royal* and *Formidable* and the ships suffered no loss from this quarter, although one of the transports, the *Empire Song*, was sunk by mines on 9 May. The remainder reached Alexandria, carrying the surviving 238 tanks and 43 Hurricanes.

Admiral Sir James Somerville's Force H had scarcely returned to Gibraltar when, on 21 May, it was required to undertake Operation *Splice*, involving the flying-off of forty-eight more Malta-bound Hurricanes from the carriers *Ark Royal* and *Furious*. All these aircraft arrived safely, providing a much-needed boost for the island's air defences. This was followed, on 6 June, by Operation *Rocket*, in which the same two carriers flew off another thirty-five Hurricanes, led by Blenheim bombers from Gibraltar, and on 14 June by Operation *Tracer*, in which *Ark Royal* and *Victorious* launched forty-seven more Hurricanes from a point south of the Balearics, led on this occasion by four Lockheed Hudsons. Four of this latest batch failed to reach Malta.

All these facts were known to Armstrong, who had received a through briefing on the situation in the Mediterranean theatre before leaving England and who had been brought completely up to date during his short stay in Gibraltar. The latest news was that, after pounding Malta for the past five months, the German dive-bomber squadrons had suddenly departed from Sicily, leaving the Italian Air Force alone to carry on the air offensive against the island fortress.

The news had not come as a surprise to Armstrong, who remembered a prediction made some months earlier by his Polish flight commander, Stanislaw Kalinski. Once the Germans had given up all hope of launching a successful invasion of Britain, the Pole had said, they would turn south and east, first of all invading the Balkans to secure their southern flank, and then launching a massive attack on the Soviet Union. The fact that the Nazis had a non-aggression treaty with the USSR meant nothing.

Armstrong was convinced, now, that Kalinski was

right, and that an invasion of Russia was about to take place. The *Luftwaffe* units must have been withdrawn from Sicily to support it, at least in its early stages. He had no doubt, though, that they would be back.

"Quite a sight, isn't it?"

The voice at his elbow made Armstrong start. He turned to see his second-in-command, Lieutenant Commander Jamie Baird – known to his colleagues as Dickie – standing a couple of paces behind him, his elbow resting on a Hurricane's wing. Baird was dressed in a crisply-laundered white uniform; a pair of binoculars hung round his neck.

Armstrong knew what the naval officer meant. The *Ark Royal*'s escorting warships did indeed make a splendid sight; especially the great battlecruiser HMS *Renown*, 32,000 tons of sheer power, creaming through the water with her lesser sisters, the cruiser *Hermione* and six destroyers. The *Renown* packed a formidable punch: 6 fifteen-inch guns, 20 four-point-fives and 24 two-pounder anti-aircraft guns. She was old, having been launched in 1916, but she was more than a match for anything the Italian Navy could send against her – thanks to the efforts of a handful of Fairey Swordfish crews of the Fleet Air Arm, who had crippled Italy's capital ships in a daring torpedo attack at Taranto in November 1940.

Armstrong turned to speak to his friend, then peered up into the southern sky, where a sudden glint of light had attracted his attention. It was a distant aircraft, its wings reflecting the rays of the rising sun. It seemed to be heading towards the convoy. Armstrong pointed it out to Baird, who trained his glasses on it.

The aircraft was still a long way off. "Can't quite make it out," Baird said. "Oh, wait a minute . . . I can see it better now. It's turned, and there's not so much light reflection. Twin-engined, single fin and rudder . . . slim fuselage. I'm pretty certain it's a Maryland."

"Let's have a look." Baird handed the binoculars to Armstrong, who focused on the aircraft just as it turned back towards the convoy.

"It's a Maryland, all right," he said after a few moments. "One of the Vichy French aircraft out on a recce, I should think."

The Martin Maryland bomber-reconnaissance aircraft was an American type, originally ordered by the French Air Force in 1939. Some had been delivered in time to see action against the Germans in the summer of 1940, and when France collapsed most of the survivors had been flown to North Africa. Those not yet delivered to the French had been taken over by the RAF and mostly served with squadrons in the Middle East; it was a Maryland, operating from Malta, that had photographed the Italian fleet in Taranto harbour before the Fleet Air Arm attack.

The Maryland continued its approach, then circled for a while out of gun range before flying off in the direction of Algeria. Armstrong handed the binoculars back to Baird.

"I don't like the look of that," he said, gazing after the rapidly receding aircraft. "I wouldn't put it past the Vichy French to have a crack at us in retaliation for

Syria. We'd better keep our eyes peeled for a while after take-off, especially when we're passing Bizerta."

French fighters from North Africa, he knew, had already made close approaches to RAF aircraft flying to Malta, and the Allied campaign in Syria had complicated matters. A couple of weeks earlier, British Empire and Free French forces had invaded the Vichy French territories of Syria and the Lebanon to secure them against Axis intervention and so forestall a potential threat to the Suez Canal zone. Heavy fighting was still in progress, and the Allies were gaining the upper hand, but the French in Algeria might just decide that honour was at stake and take some sort of armed action in support of their colleagues at the other end of the Mediterranean.

Baird was not as well informed as Armstrong on the military situation in North Africa.

"What have they got over there?" he wanted to known. "In the way of fighters, I mean."

Armstrong thought for a moment. He had been in France in the last days of June 1940, just before the armistice was signed, and had a rough idea how many aircraft the French had managed to evacuate.

"They've got about a hundred and forty Curtiss Hawks," he told the Fleet Air Arm pilot, "and I reckon they're the most dangerous. They put up a good fight in France, but they're probably suffering from a shortage of spares by now. Still, they could be troublesome." Armstrong had flown and fought in the American-built P-36A Hawk during his brief spell with the French, and had developed an affection for the tubby little radial-engined fighter.

"Apart from them," he continued, "there'll be about a hundred and fifty Dewoitine 520s. They're nippy, too, and roughly in the same class as the Hurricane. Say three hundred fighters in all, perhaps two-thirds of them serviceable at any one time. You can add a similar number of bombers to the total, I suppose, some of them modern types. Enough to give us problems, at any rate."

"Or to give us a substantial helping hand if they so choose," Baird snorted. "Instead of sitting on their backsides, the French in North Africa could be attacking the Germans and Italians in the rear, and helping us to stop the enemy's supply convoys getting across the Mediterranean. If only they'd taken the right decision last year . . ."

His words trailed away, and Armstrong knew what he was thinking. In July 1940 Admiral Gensoul, the commander of the French Fleet – which had taken refuge in the North African ports of Oran and Mers-el-Kebir – had been given a series of stark choices by the British government. If he refused to join forces with the British, or to sail his fleet to a British port or to the West Indies, or to scuttle his vessels within six hours of the ultimatum, then his warships would be destroyed.

Admiral Gensoul had refused, and as a consequence Admiral Somerville's Force H had attacked, destroying one French battleship and seriously damaging two others, together with other lesser craft. Over 1,200 French sailors had died. It was an action, carried out on the direct orders of Winston Churchill, that had not exactly endeared the British to the Vichy French.

But the alternative would have been the possible seizure of a very powerful naval force by the enemy, and an Axis victory in the Mediterranean. And for besieged Britain, that would have meant the end.

Armstrong sighed and glanced at his watch. "Come on, Dickie. Let's have some breakfast. Time's getting on, and it's going to be a long day."

Breakfast was already being served when they reached the wardroom. They looked around and quickly spotted Kalinski, who waved them towards some vacant chairs. There were two other RAF officers at the table, both members of Armstrong's Special Duties Squadron; they were Flight Lieutenant Eamonn O'Day, whose name left no doubt about his ethnic origins, and Pilot Officer Piet van Berg, a South African.

"What's on the menu?" Armstrong asked, sitting down opposite Kalinski. The Pole made a face. "Corn flakes with reconstituted milk, bacon with reconstituted eggs, toast and marmalade. And coffee. Plenty of coffee, thank God."

Armstrong grinned, well aware that Kalinski considered himself to be something of an epicure. "Well, Stan, you'd better make the most of it. Heaven only knows how long it will be before we see another decent breakfast."

Reconstituted or not, the food was actually very good, and there was plenty of it. Halfway through the meal a sub lieutenant appeared at Armstrong's elbow.

"Wing Commander Armstrong, sir? Hope you're enjoying your breakfast. We usually have bream on a Saturday, and that would have given you a pretty thirsty send-off.

We'll be at the flying-off position in one hour; take-off at oh-seven-oh-five."

Armstrong nodded and reached for his coffee cup, glancing over the rim at Baird. Since no Hudson or Blenheim was available to navigate the Hurricane formation to Malta, he had picked Baird – who had a vast amount of experience of over-water flying – to lead. Armstrong would fly as the naval officer's number two, cross-checking the navigation as they went along.

They had been through the drill several times since leaving Gibraltar, so that each of the twenty-four Hurricane pilots knew exactly what to expect on the perilous trip. The Hurricanes would by flying in six flights of four; they were to form up as quickly as possible after take-off, to conserve precious fuel, and when they were all in position the ship would flash a white light, the signal for them to set course.

After breakfast, Armstrong, as senior RAF officer, assembled the pilots on deck and issued a few last-minute instructions and cautions. He told them about the French reconnaissance aircraft, warning them to be on the lookout for Vichy fighters off Bizerta; they must also be especially cautious and alert when passing the island of Pantellaria, for the Italians were known to have a squadron of fighters there.

Armstrong glanced at his watch; it was 06.50. "All right," he said, "I hope everybody's had a good pee." The remark brought some chuckles, but they all knew the importance of it. They would be airborne for three and a half hours, flying at the best economical speed;

they would be stiff and cramped and soaked in sweat in their small, functional cockpits, and the pain of a swollen bladder added to that would make the flight sheer hell. Armstrong, as a former Spitfire photo-reconnaissance pilot, had had personal experience of that particular misery on long, lonely flights deep into Germany, and the dinghy pack on which a pilot sat felt as solid as concrete after a while; it was impossible to get comfortable, no matter how much one squirmed.

"Cockpits in five minutes, chaps," Armstrong announced, then turned to have a word with the ground crews, who had been standing in a small knot some distance apart, looking on, waiting to see off the aircraft and pilots. They had worked incredibly hard over the past few days; the Hurricanes had come to them in pieces, packed in crates, and within a week they had assembled them, working in the cramped conditions of *Ark Royal*'s hangar, with only inches to spare between one aircraft and its neighbour. It was a necessary move, for German and Italian agents abounded on the Spanish mainland, logging and reporting everything that passed through Gibraltar. Only after the aircraft carrier had sailed, and The Rock had receded beyond the horizon, had the aircraft been brought up on deck.

Since then, the mechanics had adjusted and tested the fighters' Rolls-Royce Merlin engines, hydraulics, electrical and compressed-air systems, oxygen, instruments and guns. The aircraft were Mk IIA Hurricanes, which carried the same armament of eight Browning 0.303 machine-guns as the earlier Mk I; the main differences were that the Mk IIA was fitted with a more powerful

Merlin XX engine of 1,260 horsepower and a pair of 44-gallon underwing fuel tanks, a vital addition for the flight to Malta.

Armstrong made a special point of thanking the engine fitters for their efforts, for engine failure was a nightmare possibility that lurked at the back of every pilot's mind. The single-engined fighter pilot who enjoyed flying over water for long distances hadn't been born, and if you had to ditch on this particular trip there would be no one around to fish you out.

The pilots climbed into their aircraft, strapped themselves in and settled down as comfortably as they could as the last few minutes before take-off ticked away. Armstrong noticed that the warships escorting the carrier were zig-zagging continuously, an insurance against any prowling enemy submarines. He didn't know whether the Germans had any U-boats in the Mediterranean, but the Italians certainly had.

The Hurricanes were ranged along the edge of the flight deck, twelve on either side, facing diagonally inwards at an angle towards the bow. Armstrong's eyes, for the moment, were on a man in a yellow skull cap, balancing on the deck in front of the lines of aircraft. He carried a checkered flag, which he now raised; it was the signal for the first four pilots, of which Armstrong was one, to start their engines.

Armstrong's engine coughed into life, caught first go, and was soon roaring with an encouragingly healthy sound. Opposite him, two of the flight deck crew seized the wingtips of Baird's aircraft and swung its nose towards the bow as the pilot taxied out from his station. A moment later the men jumped clear and the Hurricane forged ahead, gathering speed until it lifted off and rose cleanly above the bow. It had been a perfect take-off, born of long experience.

Now it was Armstrong's turn. Assisted by the two sailors, he lined up on the centreline of the flight deck, scanning his instruments to make sure that all the temperature and pressure needles were in their right positions and checking that the propellor blades were set to fine pitch, which would give them the necessary 'bite'. Some pilots had been known to try to take off in coarse pitch, which did not work, with predictably embarrassing results.

Armstrong held the Hurricane on its brakes and opened the throttle slowly, the fighter vibrating as power surged through. Out of the corner of his eye, he saw the man make a downwards motion with the checkered flag. The pilot released the brakes and the Hurricane surged forward. He pushed the control column hard forward and the tail came up at once. He could see where he was going now and had no difficulty in keeping the aircraft straight, aiming the nose to the right of a marker flag that had been set up in the forward anti-aircraft position.

The grey tower of the carrier's 'island' flashed past. The deck now looked even shorter than it had earlier that morning; the bow dipped and Armstrong had a frightening glimpse of the glistening Mediterranean through the shimmering arc of his propeller. Ruddering carefully to keep the aircraft straight, he eased back the stick as the Hurricane reached flying speed and she bounced into the air, aided by the combined speed of the carrier's twenty knots and a fifteen-knot headwind that was blowing straight from the east.

There was a brief eddy of turbulence, then the bow fell away behind and he pushed the stick forward ever so slightly, gently lowering the nose to gain an extra few knots. The speed built up comfortably and he pulled back the stick again, his other hand holding the throttle wide open, and brought the Hurricane round in a broad climbing turn, briefly relinquishing his hold on the throttle to raise the undercarriage and flaps. He heard the wheels click home into their wells under the wings and the red light showed that they had locked.

At a thousand feet he changed over to the auxiliary fuel tanks, the engine and his heart both missing a beat as he did so. Then the Merlin resumed its normal smooth running and he relaxed a little as he curved round to join up with Baird, whose aircraft he could see ahead of him, some 500 feet higher up.

He circled the carrier, gaining height all the time, thinking how small the ships of the fleet looked, even from 1,500 feet. It was small wonder that bombs missed them. He wondered what chance he would have of landing back on the carrier, should his engine fail. There had been a time during the Norwegian campaign, in June 1940, when a whole squadron of Hurricanes had successfully landed on HMS *Glorious* after being evacuated from Narvik; a tremendous feat that had turned to tragedy when the carrier had been sunk with the loss of almost everyone on board by the battlecruisers *Scharnhorst* and *Gneisenau*.

A few minutes later the question became academic as the other Hurricane flights joined up and the white light flashed from the carrier, sending the whole formation off towards Malta.

The Hurricanes climbed to 8,000 feet and settled down on a steady course into the glare of the rising sun, the ochre mountains of Algeria's coastal range visible to starboard. All the pilots wore smoked-glass goggles, but the burnished ball of the sun stabbed painfully at their eyeballs nonetheless.

After an hour's flying a thin haze crept down on the horizon, born out of the rising sun's heat, and soon the African coastline turned blue in colour. The formation cruised steadily on past Galite Island, about twenty miles off the mainland; a solitary lighthouse was the only sign of habitation, and the sea breaking against steep cliffs gave the place a lonely, forbidding appearance. At Bizerta – with no sign at all of Vichy French fighters – the distant mountains began to recede inland; at the same time the haze began to disperse, and soon they were flying in perfect conditions, with seemingly endless visibility.

Armstrong leaned forward a little in the cockpit, peering at a dark smudge that had materialised on the horizon. He quickly identified it as Cape Bon, the northernmost tip of Tunisia, and smiled to himself, pleased with Baird's navigational skill.

Baird, followed by the rest of the formation, altered course slightly to the south-east, on a track that should take the Hurricanes safely clear of Pantellaria. They could see that island now; Armstrong thought it looked a little like the Isle of Man, with a mountain at its southern end and a low-lying plain to the north. There was no sign of enemy fighters, but Armstrong reached up and pulled back the cockpit hood to give himself a better view, feeling rejuvenated and coming fully alert as the sudden blast of air plucked at him.

The rocky cone of Pantellaria slid by without incident. The sun was quite high by now, the sky and the sea beneath a vivid blue. The visibility was excellent, and away to the right Armstrong could see the white blur of a town on the coast of Tunisia; a glance at his map told him that it was Susa. A small convoy appeared to be heading for it, each ship trailing a herringbone of wake.

A red light winked on the instrument panel, prompting Armstrong to switch over to the main fuel tank. Malta was not more than an hour's flying time away, so the fuel situation was reassuring.

Yet as the minutes ticked by, Armstrong could not help but feel a twinge of anxiety. It gave way to relief when, dead ahead, a small section of the horizon seemed to change colour. He blinked to make sure that his eyes were not playing tricks, but there was no mistaking the dark patch that rose from the sea – or rather two dark patches, the smaller one closer to the incoming fighters. That would be Gozo, with Malta beyond it.

As the Hurricanes drew nearer, the dark hue of the islands gave way to a russet colour; it was as though someone had tossed a couple of giant autumn leaves on the water. More details emerged as the aircraft began a gradual descent; Armstrong picked out steep cliffs, and beyond them a spider's web of white lines that were stone walls meandering across the surface of Gozo. There were houses, too, sometimes in clusters, all of them white. Throughout the entire flight there had been total radio silence. Malta's radar would have picked up the Hurricane formation while it was still a long way out to sea, and would have been monitoring its progress on the final approach to the island. Now the radio burst into sudden life, making Armstrong start.

"All Upwood aircraft pancake Luqa, I repeat, all Upwood aircraft pancake Luqa. Do not land at Takali. Do not land at Takali."

'Upwood' was the Hurricane formation's callsign. Something was clearly amiss, because the original plan had called for half the aircraft to land at Takali and the rest at Luqa. The aircraft were down to 4,000 feet now, still descending. They sped across Gozo and over the blue channel that separated the two main islands. There was a third, tiny island in the channel; Armstrong discovered later that its name was Comino.

The whole of Malta was clearly visible now, its features etched in sharp focus. As they crossed the coast, Armstrong noticed a strange, hazy pillar, like sand-coloured smoke, slanting up towards the sun, as though the core of the island were being dragged up to meet the sky. With a sudden shock he realised that he was looking at the dust kicked up by dozens of bomb bursts, drifting slowly on a light breeze. Malta was under heavy air attack, and they were flying right into the middle of it.

Three

apitano Umberto Ricci of the Italian Air Force, looking down from the vantage point of his Macchi C.200 fighter 15,000 feet above Malta, did not share Armstrong's view that the twin islands resembled russet-coloured autumn leaves. In his opinion, they looked for all the world like two lumps of horse shit. But then, Ricci did not like Malta, nor did he like the Maltese. The southern English, he called them. He knew, of course, that there were those on Malta who were sympathetic to Mussolini's fascist Italy – some who were even prepared to act as spies on its behalf – but the great majority were solidly pro-British. For the life of him, he could not understand why.

Look at what was happening to them now because of that attitude, he thought, as he watched the impeccable formation of bombers cruising along a few thousand feet below. There were thirty of them, Savoia SM.79s, flying in five tight arrowheads of six aircraft, one flight behind the other. Even as he watched, bombs were falling from the leading aircraft, curving down to explode on the airfield at Takali. But his eyes, he told himself, should not be on the bombers; they should be on the lookout for the British fighters that would be somewhere in the vicinity, climbing into the sun, waiting for the right moment to attack.

They would not attack just yet, for the volume of flak being hurled up from the surface of the island was fearsome. The gunners had predicted the height at which the bombers were flying – 12,000 feet – with great accuracy, and their formation was almost obscured by the drifting clouds of shell bursts. How the pilots managed to hold a steady course through all that, Ricci did not know. He was glad that he was a fighter pilot.

One of the bombers in the second flight was hit. It fell slowly out of formation, its fuel tanks ablaze, and turned over on its back, plunging towards the island, its doom marked by a dense streamer of black smoke. Ricci did not see any parachutes.

The bombers were escorted by twenty-seven fighters; Ricci's own 15th Squadron, plus two squadrons of Fiat CR.42 biplanes. Ricci had flown Fiats previously, and in many ways preferred them to the Macchis with which his squadron was now equipped. For one thing, they were more manoeuvrable. But although they could hold their own against the British Gloster Gladiator biplanes which the Italians had encountered in Greece and North Africa, they were no match for the Hawker Hurricane; and against the Spitfire, they were dead meat.

Ricci knew that all too well. In October 1940, he had been a pilot with the ill-fated Italian Air Corps which Mussolini, eager to participate in the great air battle that was supposed to have paved the way for the invasion and defeat of Britain, had sent to Belgium. Italian bombers, escorted by CR.42s and Fiat G.50 fighters, had made several attacks on British coastal targets and wild claims had been made about the number of British fighters destroyed. In fact, no British aircraft had been shot down by the Italians at all; the RAF, on the other hand, had shot the Italians out of the sky in considerable numbers, and at the end of the year the Air Corps had returned to its homeland with its tail between its legs, accompanied by not a few derisory remarks from its German allies, who had not wanted the Italians there in the first place.

The bombers had completed their attack and were now turning for home. Ricci, whose squadron was leading the fighter escort, now took the latter into a wide turn, intent on positioning it between the retreating bombers and the dangerous sun, out of which the Hurricanes must surely come.

He was not disappointed. A few seconds later, four Hurricanes came hurtling through the Italian fighter formation at what seemed incredible speed, firing as they went. Ricci opened the throttle wide and went after them, cursing as he lost sight of them behind the Macchi's massive radial engine, knowing that he had no chance at all of catching them. He put his aircraft into a climbing turn, seeing as he did so other fighters harrying the bombers, which were now little more than specks in the northern sky. Two of the Savoias were already trailing smoke, but were managing to hold their position in the formation. One of the Hurricanes had been hit, too; it turned upside down and a dark bundle fell from the cockpit, dropping a considerable distance before a white streamer of parachute silk became visible.

Ricci had no time to see whether the parachute had opened fully. His sole purpose now was to break up the British fighter attack before it could inflict more damage on the bombers. But now the four original Hurricanes had reappeared and were in the thick of things, attacking the Italian fighters from the flank. Within seconds the sky was a melee of flashing, twisting aircraft.

Ricci managed to get off a fleeting shot at a Hurricane, which missed, and wished wholeheartedly that his aircraft carried a more powerful armament than its two nose-mounted 12.7mm Breda machine-guns. You had to be very lucky, or very expert, to be successful. The Hurricanes, with their eight machine-guns, were much better armed.

The battle was spread out all over the sky now, and Ricci's attempts to get on the tail of another Hurricane had brought him down to just a few thousand feet above the sea, to the east of Gozo. Suddenly, he sighted a formation of aircraft heading towards Gozo, and quickly identified them as Hurricanes. The thought never crossed his mind that the incoming aircraft might be reinforcements for the island, that they had probably been airborne for several hours, and therefore would have no fuel to spare for combat.

Erring on the side of discretion, he radioed his pilots, ordering them to catch up with the bombers and return to their base at Crotone, on Sicily. He could almost smell the coffee that would be waiting for them.

Armstrong and his fellow Hurricane pilots, aware now

of the air combat taking place off Malta, continued their approach to Luqa. They passed over Takali airfield, wheels and landing flaps lowered, and saw smoke mingling with the dust that rose from it. Several objects, presumably aircraft, were burning on the ground. Some bombs also appeared to have fallen on Grand Harbour, whose deep gash lay over on the left, with its tiers of white, flat-roofed houses and its multitude of baroque churches, yellow and soft against the sea, clustered all around it.

Luqa was dead ahead, its face ravaged by the smallpox of bomb craters; troops and civilians were at work, filling them in. The Hurricanes roared overhead, breaking into the circuit to land in line astern. Glancing up, Armstrong spotted a couple more Hurricanes circling watchfully overhead, covering the newcomers while they landed.

The newly-arrived pilots continued to fly around the circuit as they queued up to approach the only runway that still looked reasonably intact, the shadows of their aircraft fleeting over the grey-green landscape, the white walls and stunted trees. There was no time for the nicety of the flight leaders holding off to let their men land first; it was a matter of getting down quickly, starting with the first to arrive. Armstrong gave a quick glance above and behind, a roll of the head to make sure that there was nothing sinister on his tail, and throttled back, fishtailing to reduce speed.

A couple of hundred yards ahead, he saw Dickie Baird touch down in a cloud of dust and pebbles. Then it was his own turn. His Hurricane slid over some heaps of stone, the shattered wreck of an aircraft and a gravel track. He flared out gently, easing back the stick and closing the throttle in one movement. The wheels touched, the Hurricane bounced lightly then settled down, rolling forward along the sun-baked strip.

Armstrong looked around him, having no idea where to go next. Luqa was a scene of utter confusion, with Hurricanes taxying everywhere along bits of runway and winding tracks that disappeared into blast pens. Men in nondescript bits of uniform ran to and fro, apparently aimlessly, although in fact each had a job to do. Some of them were mounted on bicycles, and one of these suddenly swung in front of Armstrong's aircraft, looking over his shoulder and beckoning. The pilot saw that the man carried a large placard on his back, with the words 'Follow Me' on it.

He did so, weaving the nose from side to side so that the cyclist would not be obscured by the long engine cowling. The cyclist led him off the runway onto one of the makeshift taxi tracks, guiding the Hurricane around piles of stones which, Armstrong discovered, were distributed all around the airfield in readiness to fill in bomb craters.

At the end of the track a blast pen had been built, its walls constructed from sandbags and sand-filled petrol cans. The cyclist signalled to him to halt just short of it and, before he had time to make another move, he found himself practically lifted from the cockpit by a couple of burly airmen, one of whom switched off the fighter's engine. As Armstrong jumped stiffly down from the wing, his head aching, already conscious of the heat, three more airmen seized the Hurricane

by its tail and swung it round, dragging it backwards
into the pen so that its nose was pointing out towards
the airfield.

Armstrong saw that the ground crews consisted of
soldiers as well as airmen. It seemed that on Malta,
everybody mucked in.

The pilot thankfully stripped off his Mae West lifejacket,
a move that revealed the rank badges on the epaulettes of
his shirt. One of the deeply sunburned airmen glanced at
them and grinned at him.

"Sorry about all the rush, sir. Got to get 'em turned
round quick, like, in case another raid comes in. There'll
be some transport along in a minute or two," he added.

Armstrong nodded and stepped deftly out of the way
while soldiers and airmen converged on the Hurricane
from all directions, staggering under the weight of cans of
fuel. Someone removed the gun panels with a screwdriver
and heaved out Armstrong's kitbag, which he tossed
unceremoniously into the dust. The pilot collected it,
then looked on in astonishment as an airman produced
cartons of cigarettes, a box of what looked like medical
supplies, assorted tools and a mosquito net from the other
guns bays. Armstrong had had no inlking that they were
there, but it was clear that not an inch to room had been
wasted.

Armstrong wandered out of the blast pen, away from
all the turmoil, and waited for the promised transport.
After a while an ancient bus, its sides dented and
riddled with holes, screeched to a stop outside the
pen. Someone waved to him from the doorway; he
saw that it was Baird and trotted across, throwing his

kitbag inside and clambering aboard after it, the Fleet Air Arm pilot lending a helping hand.

"Some welcome," Baird said unsmilingly. Armstrong clung to a handrail as the bus lurched away with a crash of gears.

"Well, we're stuck with it for a day or two," he said, looking round. All the pilots who had flown in from the *Ark Royal* were on the bus; he had been the last to be picked up. Of the twenty-four new arrivals, nineteen would remain on the island. He and the four pilots who formed the nucleus of the Special Duty Squadron would fly on to Alexandria, as soon as an aircraft arrived to take them there. More pilots were to join them in Egypt, bringing the squadron up to full strength.

The bus careered around the airfield perimeter, its occupants hanging on grimly as the driver – an ancient, wizened Maltese with a grimy sweat rag tied around his neck – swerved around craters and mounds of rubble. Through the glassless windows Armstrong caught sight of more blast pens, some empty, others containing the burnt-out remains of aircraft. A Wellington bomber hung over the edge of one of them like a stranded whale, its back broken.

There was a shattering roar overhead and the pilots peered out of the windows, craning their necks to see what was going on. Hurricanes were taking off in rapid succession, whipping up their wheels and flaps and climbing hard towards the north.

The bus driver put his foot down for another few hundred yards, then came to a halt beside a heavy anti-aircraft site. Everyone piled out to see what was happening, staring towards the north. It was Kalinski who spotted the raiders first; a speck seemed to pop out of nowhere, as though emerging from a hole in the sky, followed by another and another. Eventually eighteen were visible, with a few more distant specks that must be their escorting fighters weaving above and behind them.

The enemy aircraft were close enough to be identified now, and Armstrong was puzzled. They were Junkers Ju 87 *Stukas*.

"I thought the Germans had pulled out of Sicily," he said, to no one in particular.

"Maybe they left the Italians some of their dive-bombers," Kalinski said. In fact, the Polish pilot was almost right; enough Ju 87s had been delivered to the Italian Air Force late in 1940 to equip four groups, two of which were based on Sicily on a rotational basis for operations against Malta. The RAF pilots watched, now, as the *Stukas* cruised overhead, seemingly untroubled by the anti-aircraft barrage, then peeled off one by one to dive on their objective, which was obviously Takali. There was no sign of any Hurricanes; the enemy fighter escort must be keeping them busy.

The thump of bombs hitting Takali aerodrome made the ground reverberate. The dust clouds, already becoming a familiar sight, rose in the distance. Pursued by the AA fire, each *Stuka* pulled out of its screaming dive and raced away northwards. The gunners claimed one *Stuka*; it released its bomb but failed to level out, continuing its near-vertical plunge until it hit the ground in a fountain of smoke and dust.

The last of the raiders sped away. Somewhere in the distance, a siren wailed the all-clear. The pilots climbed back on the bus, which resumed its rickety journey to its unknown destination, pulling laboriously up a hill. Looking out to the right Armstrong saw a flat expanse of ground, a hillside broken by the dark, yawning mouths of caves, and some sandbagged emplacements, with a huge pall off dust hanging over everything. That was Takali. An acrid stench drifted into the bus, making its occupants cough.

The bus churned its way up the hill, twisting around bends, and suddenly the shadows of high walls fell across it. The driver threaded his way deftly through narrow streets, some of them showing signs of bomb damage, and through occasional openings Armstrong caught tantalising glimpses of ancient, curved archways and baroque churches. He wondered where the place was, and Dickie Baird answered his unspoken question.

"This is Rabat," he said unexpectedly. "It's the old capital of Malta. It used to be called Melita – that's where the island gets its name from – and, according to legend, Saint Paul stayed here after he was shipwrecked."

Armstrong looked at his deputy in surprise. "Dickie, you never cease to amaze me. Have you been here before? You never said."

Baird smiled. "Been here a few times, as a matter of fact," he admitted. "What naval officer hasn't?"

The road narrowed even more and the bus passed slowly through an archway, a gate into some inner sanctum enclosed by vast stone walls.

"We're in M'dina now," Baird continued. "These

walls were built by the Arabs to fortify Melita when they occupied the place after the Romans had gone, and the bit left outside, which you've just seen, they called Rabat; the name simply means 'suburb'. When the Spaniards occupied the island they changed M'dina's name to *Citta Notabile*. Then the Knights Hospitallers came along and made Malta their HQ, so to speak; they built Valletta, which is really one big fortress, and moved the capital there. After that M'dina took second place, but to many Maltese it's still the capital; they call it the *Citta Vecchia*, or Old City."

Armstrong, always fascinated by history, was about to put some questions to Baird when the bus halted outside a palace, its sunlit walls the colour of honey. It boasted a massive iron-bound double door. They piled out of the bus and went through the door into the palace, their shoes kicking up small clouds of the grey dust that lay like a mantle over everything as they went. As they went inside Armstrong shivered slightly. The gloom of the big hall was dank and forbidding, in sharp contrast to the hot sunlight outside. Once, he thought, the whole place must have been filled with light and laughter; now its walls held only the musty odour of dead dynasties.

A Royal Air Force officer, a squadron leader, was there to meet them. He singled out Armstrong by the latter's rank badges and came across, extending a hand.

"Hello, sir. I'm Harrison. Glad you made it all right. Would you mind waiting here with your chaps for a minute or two? The rest are going upstairs for a briefing. It's the procedure with new pilots. We like them to know what's what, from the word go. Won't be long."

Finding the gloomy hall depressing, Armstrong and his fellow pilots went back outside into the sunlight and chatted idly while they waited for Harrison's return. He was back within five minutes.

"I expect you could all do with a drink," he said. "We've a bar upstairs. Not much in it, I'm afraid; just a few bottles of Cisk, the local brew, but it's better than nothing.

A few minutes later, clutching bottles of beer that proved surprisingly cool and refreshing, having made some proper introductions and dropped their kit in rooms that had been assigned to them, they stepped out of the small room that served as the Mess bar on to a spacious flat roof. From it they could see the whole eastern part of Malta, laid out below like a relief model. Directly ahead were Grand Harbour and Slima Creek, with Valletta nestling between them, and the five towns of Vittoriosa, Senglea, Cospicua, Floriana and Slima grouped around in a semi-circle; to one side of them Luqa, where the Hurricanes had recently landed, could be clearly identified by its runway pattern; beyond it lay Hal Far airfield and the naval base of Kalafrana; and in the foreground was Takali, with a haze of smoke and dust still drifting from it.

"Nice view, isn't it?" Harrison said. "Pity the Huns and the Eyeties had to go and spoil it. By the way, you've probably heard a lot of bloody nonsense about the Italians. Our experience here has shown that they'll often stay and fight while the Germans are high-tailing it for home. Any of you met the Italians?"

"Flight Lieutenant Kalinski and I have," Armstrong

said. "In France, just before the armistice. As you say, they are not to be underestimated."

Harrison glanced up at the sky. "Well, I reckon they'll leave us alone for a bit. They're fairly predictable; they'll come over before lunch, then take the afternoon off. They sometimes send a small raid in around teatime, and one or two more during the night. Things are nothing like as hectic as they were before the Germans pulled out, though."

Armstrong cleared his throat. The cool beer was carving a very pleasant passage through the dust that lined it.

"What about getting us to Egypt?" he asked abruptly. "As I understood it, we were to deliver the Hurricanes, and then an aircraft would be available to take us on the last leg to Alexandria."

Harrison's face adopted a mysterious expression. "Oh, it will, sir. It will. Not before tomorrow, though, I'm afraid. It's, er, otherwise engaged at the moment. Can't tell you any more than that for the time being. But never fear – you won't be here long enough to catch The Dog."

Armstrong raised a questioning eyebrow.

"The Malta Dog," Harrison explained. "It's a particularly nasty form of amoebic dysentery. Malta's one of the most highly fertilised places in the world, you see, and since there's a shortage of animal fertiliser, guess what they use. You're OK if you don't drink the local milk – it's goat's milk, by the way – but we have no alternative. The Dog can make life absolute hell, but one gets used to it."

They had lunch, which consisted of bully beef and reconstituted mashed potatoes. Afterwards, while Kalinski, O'Day and van Berg lazed in the rooftop sun, for want of anything better to do, Armstrong decided to make an excursion into Valletta, and Baird volunteered to go with him. They hitched a lift in the back of an Army ration truck that was heading for the main harbour, following the hot, dusty road that led over an open plain through Birkirkara, with its cluster of white, flat-roofed houses; Baird said that the Maltese kept chickens on the roofs, if they were short of space on the ground. Small villages appeared and then vanished just as quickly behind the dust-cloud as the truck sped on, and then the landscape changed abruptly as the vehicle passed through the arches of an aqueduct and buildings began to appear on either side.

"Hamrun," Baird announced. "C'mon, Ken – we can walk from here."

The driver, a cheery corporal in the Royal Malta Artillery, obligingly stopped to let the two men off. Dusting themselves down, they gazed at their surroundings. They had disembarked on the edge of what appeared to be ornamental gardens of some sort – or at least that was what they might have been, before the army took over. They were now the site of a battery of anti-aircraft guns, their long barrels pointing skywards over the town of Floriana towards the deepwater inlets of Grand Harbour.

Floriana had taken a good deal of bomb damage, made worse by the fact that the buildings, constructed mainly from blocks of soft limestone, had proved incapable of withstanding bomb blast. The shock waves had crushed them like eggs, choking the streets with mountains of collapsed masonry through which lanes had recently been cleared.

The pilots walked on through the stony wilderness, past gangs of Maltese workmen labouring in the debris under a pale yellow shroud of dust. Armstrong and Baird were careful to keep to the middle of the road, for there were empty shells of buildings on either side, their walls cracked and leaning at all sorts of odd angles. One of them, taller than the rest, caught Armstrong's attention and he stopped, gazing at it in fascination. Its external walls had crumbled away completely, stripped off by some mysterious trick of blast, but the walls of the rooms inside were still intact. It looked like a house of cards, capped crazily by what was left of the roof. Broken and splintered furniture was still inside, piled haphazardly in the corners, and here and there a torn lace curtain fluttered, caught on some jagged outcrop of stone.

"Gives you the creeps, doesn't it?" Baird commented as they stood and stared. "I wonder who lived there?"

"Well," Armstrong retorted, "whoever it was they certainly aren't living there now. Come on, for God's sake, before the bloody place falls down on top of us."

They turned into a narrow lane, a defile sliced through the living rock that plunged steeply down towards the harbour. It was shady here, and the doors and windows of houses gaped at them, dark caverns of gloom in which they could sense movement. The bombs had done their work here, too, as scattered blocks of stone and pock-marked walls testified, but most of the buildings were still intact, the depth of the street having sheltered them from the worst of the onslaught. As the pilots descended towards the rectangle of light that marked the far end of the alley they encountered growing numbers of people, most of them converging on a single shop outside of which black-clad women stood in a long queue, waiting patiently. The whole shop front was open to the street and Armstrong peered in as they went past, catching a glimpse of an enormously fat woman weighing rations on a set of ancient iron scales. Some of the women glanced with brief curiosity at the two men, then looked away disinterestedly. Armstrong was reminded of the 'business as usual' signs outside battered shops in London's bombed-out East End, and of the 'London can take it' slogans chalked on the walls. Malta was taking it, too, with magnificent courage, although Armstrong could not help wondering whether the island's ordeal was only just beginning.

They emerged into the sunlight at the far end of the street and turned on to what had once been an avenue. It was still lined with the blast-shattered remnants of trees. It had become the main thoroughfare between Floriana and Valletta, for the main road that ran parallel to it was still blocked by the rubble of a recent Italian air raid. Beyond the rubble was a stone wall, with great gaps torn in it. The pilots picked their way across to it and stood at one of the gaps, looking down into one of the deep inlets of the harbour. The damage caused by German and Italian bombs was immediately apparent;

they could see the masts and funnels of sunken ships, sticking up out of the water.

A large freighter was moored at one of the quays, with cranes dipping steadily into her holds. On the quayside, ant-like figures were transferring the piles of cargo to waiting lorries.

"Must have come in during the night," Baird said. "I suppose that means the Eyeties will be paying us another visit before long. I hope they manage to get all the cargo offloaded."

"I wonder what the Templars would have made of all this," Armstrong said a while later, as they retraced their steps. Baird looked at him.

"Not Templars, Ken. They were never on Malta. That's a popular misconception. As I mentioned earlier, the Knights of Malta were – and are – the Hospitallers, the Sovereign Military Order of St John of Jerusalem, who defended Malta against the Turks in the sixteenth century, but there was a Maltese order of nobility that existed for a very long time before they arrived. The last time I was here, I made friends with a chap called de Molay; he was descended from a knight who helped Count Roger of Normandy kick the Moors out of these islands in 1090."

"Go on," Armstrong prompted, after Baird had been silent for a while.

"Well, some Maltese families can trace their ancestry back much further than that. You see, the island was a colony of the Phoenicians, who founded Carthage, for over a thousand years, and the language of Malta is Punic in origin, not a mixture of Latin and Sicilian, as many people think, so many family names are very old. Just to give you an example, one name – Melac – has its origin in the Carthiginian cult of Moloch. It's probably one of the oldest surviving names in the world."

Armstrong was beginning to see Malta and its people in a new light, and his fascination deepened when Baird told him that, according to legend, Hannibal was buried somewhere on the island.

The sirens screeched as they walked, interrupting their conversation, but it turned out to be a false alarm. Not until midnight did the raiders return, and yet again Malta trembled to the crash of explosions and the bark of anti-aircraft guns. The noise awakened Armstrong from a deep sleep. He got up, pulled on his trousers and groped his way out on to the flat roof, aided by flashes of light from the gun barrage.

From his vantage point the ragged outline of Grand Harbour, with its surrounding cluster of buildings, was clearly visible. The flashes of bombs and guns threw the distant shapes of twin-spired churches into sharp relief. Shell bursts spewed across the sky, following the direction of probing searchlight beams. Armstrong calculated that M'dina was a good ten miles from Valletta, but even at this distance the noise was terrific, the drumroll of explosions blotting out the sound of the bombers' engines.

Suddenly, something caught Armstrong's eye and he turned his head, peering into the darkness beyond St Julian's Bay, a little way up the coast from Slima. High over the sea, a stream of sparks danced in the night, flashing horizontally across the sky. He knew that he was watching a Beaufighter in action; fifteen of these aircraft, belonging to No 252 Squadron, had reached the island in May, their purpose being to counter the enemy night bombers.

The sparks flashed again, and this time a pinpoint of white light flickered at the spot where they converged. As Armstrong watched it grew in intensity, like an exploding star. The it began to fall, slowly at first and then faster. It flared brightly and split into a dozen fragments. They fell like meteors, each one trailing its own small tail of fire, to be abruptly extinguished in the blackness of the Mediterranean. Armstrong went on watching until the sound of the distant explosions died away, then went back to bed.

An hour or so later, a twin-engined aircraft approached Malta from the south-east. It was painted all black, and carried no national markings. As it drew closer to the island, it was joined by another aircraft, a Beaufighter. The pair flew on, and gradually the black-painted machine began a descent towards the moonlit waters of Kalafrana Bay.

A casual observer might have thought it odd that the Beaufighter made no attempt to attack; for the incoming aircraft was a German Heinkel 115 floatplane.

Four

Sunday, 22 June 1941: Malta

It had been another day of waiting and frustration, with not even an air raid to relieve the monotony, and no sign of the promised aircraft that was to take Armstrong and his pilots to Alexandria. Now they sat on the flat roof of the mansion, together with a few Hurricane pilots, some of them newcomers who had flown in with them the day before. Only Kalinski was missing; he had gone off to listen to the news on the radio. When he eventually returned, there was an odd expression on his face. Armstrong looked at him questioningly as he sat down in an adjacent deckchair.

"They've done it," he said quietly. "Just as I said they would. They've invaded Russia."

Suddenly everyone clustered around him, demanding more information. The Pole held up his hands, as though to ward off the barrage of questions.

"All I know is what it said on the wireless. It appears that the Germans have launched a full-scale invasion of Russia. They've attacked on an eighteen hundred mile front, from Karelia in the far north to the Ukraine.

Finnish and Romanian forces are involved, as well as German."

Kalinski fell silent. His eyes were downcast, and Armstrong knew what he must be thinking. There would be fighting in eastern Poland, which the Russians had occupied since they partitioned the country with Germany in 1939. He knew that Kalinski's family, of whom the Pole had heard nothing since his country was overrun, came from the Lublin area, which was in the east.

"If all this is true," O'Day remarked, "it means we've got an ally, at last."

Kalinski lifted his head, his eyes flashing. "Do not bank on that," he said grimly. "An ally of convenience, no doubt. But I know the Russians. They will take everything they can from us to help their war effort, and give nothing in return."

"If they keep half the German army occupied, that's enough to be going on with," Armstrong commented. "The Huns must think they've got a good chance of winning, though, otherwise they wouldn't have risked it. Would they?"

The question was addressed to no one in particular, but it was Kalinski who answered. "They have risked it for one good reason, and that is because they are running out of oil. They have the Romanian oilfields, but it is not enough. I think their plan is to capture the Caucasus oilfields, then push on down through the Middle East to attack the Canal Zone from the north."

"That's a bit of a tall order, isn't it?" Baird objected. "We've taken the wind out of their sails by going into Syria, wouldn't you say?"

"It depends on whether they can persuade Turkey to throw in her lot with them," Kalinski said. "The Turks were allies of Germany in the last war, remember, and they'd like nothing better to have their pre-1918 territories restored to them. But my guess is they'll wait to see what progress the Germans make in Russia before the winter sets in. That will be their real enemy, the Russian winter. If they don't achieve their initial objectives before then . . ." He left the sentence unfinished, staring up at an officer who had stepped on to the roof and who was now looking uncertainly at them. The newcomer wore unfamiliar badges of rank.

"Can we help you, old chap?" Armstrong asked politely.

"I am looking for Wing Commander Armstrong," the officer said, in an accent that could only be Scandinavian.

"Well, you've just found him," Armstrong said, rising to his feet. "What can I do for you?"

The officer brought himself stiffly to attention with a click of his heels. He was half a head taller than Armstrong, with a long, serious face and blond hair, receding a little.

"Sir, I am Lieutenant Erik Hansen, formerly of the Norwegian Naval Air Service, now attached to the Royal Air Force. I am assigned to you with immediate effect, and I am to fly you to Egypt tonight." Apart from the accent, Hansen's English was flawless.

"I see," Armstrong said. "Do you happen to have some sort of authorisation for all this?"

"Certainly, sir." The Norwegian fished in his shirt pocket and extracted a folded sheet of paper, which he handed to Armstrong. The latter unfolded it, studied it for a moment, and looked at the signature at the bottom. It was that of Air Commodore John Glendenning, the senior RAF officer responsible for special duties operations. In effect, he was Armstrong's immediate boss.

"I might have known it," Armstrong muttered under his breath, refolding the paper and handing it back. "So, have you arrived from England?"

The Norwegian shook his head. "No, sir, from Alexandria. Air Commodore Glendenning briefed me personally there yesterday. He is very anxious that you join him as soon as possible, sir. If I may suggest it, I shall return in one hour with transport, and take you and the other officers to the aircraft. We will take off as soon as it is dark."

Armstrong opened his mouth to ask a question, but was too late. Hanson put on his cap, which had been tucked under his arm, gave a crisp salute and turned on his heel, vanishing through the doorway into the shadows.

"Pretty efficient type," O'Day drawled, grinning at Armstrong. "I reckon he's after your job, Boss."

"He can have it," Armstrong retorted mildly. "Well, you heard what the man said. Let's grab some tea and get our kit together."

An hour later, as good as his word, Hansen returned with the promised transport, a fifteen-hundredweight Bedford lorry with 'YMCA Tea Car Serving HM Forces' emblazoned on its side and, somewhat incongruously, the letters RN in white stencilled on its door, denoting that the vehicle was, at least temporarily, in the custody of the Royal Navy.

The pilots were waiting in a small group at the entrance to the mansion, and Hansen, who was behind the wheel, indicated that they were to get into the back. They did so, and the lorry moved off along the road that led down through Siggiewi and Zurrieq towards Hal Far, beyond which lay Kalafrana. Armstrong had already guessed that they were to be transferred to North Africa by seaplane, so Kalafrana had to be their immediate destination.

The last flying boats had long since left Kalafrana for the comparative safety of Alexandria, and the base was now occupied mainly by air-sea rescue craft. The Royal Navy had once had a powerful force of warships based on Malta, including a flotilla of destroyers, but these had departed too in the face of the relentless air attacks.

But the Navy still had teeth. In the deep inlet of Lazaretto Harbour, where bomb-proof pens had been hewn out of the cliffs, lurked the small, manoeuvrable U-class boats of the Tenth Submarine Flotilla; craft with names like *Utmost, Upholder* and *Unbeaten,* manned by gallant men who sallied forth to strike at the Axis convoys on the Sicily-Tripoli-Tunisia route, or lie in wait off the main Italian naval bases in southern Italy in the hope of catching major enemy warships. Apart from a handful of RAF and Fleet Air Arm torpedo bombers, and a night striking force of Wellingtons, these were Malta's only offensive forces; but they were taking an increasing toll of enemy shipping.

Arriving at Kalafrana, Hansen took Armstrong and the others straight to a seaplane hangar, where the aircraft that was to take them to Alexandria awaited them. They stared at it in amazement. It was the first time any of them had seen a Heinkel 115 with the exception of Baird, who had shot one down on an intruder patrol in the summer of 1940, and their first reaction was one of surprise at how big it was. So this was the aircraft, Armstrong thought, that had caused so much trouble in the early months of the War, laying magnetic mines off the east coast of Britain and in the Thames estuary.

"The Norwegian Naval Air Service had half a dozen He 115s on strength when the Germans invaded my country," Hansen explained. "We had bought them from Germany only a few months earlier. We succeeded in evacuating three of them to England, and this is one of them. We have been using it to infiltrate agents into Italy, and to evacuate key personnel from the Balkan countries, flying to a pre-arranged rendezvous under cover of darkness. The bomb bay has been converted to carry up to six passengers, as I will show you."

They peered into the dark recesses of the Heinkel's bomb bay, where makeshift seats had been installed, and shuddered inwardly. Armstrong had a notion that the coming flight was going to be cramped, draughty and generally unpleasant.

He discovered that the Heinkel carried a normal crew of four – pilot, navigator, radio operator and gunner. The navigator had a position in the nose and also had a forward-firing machine-gun at his disposal; the other three sat in tandem under the long, glazed cockpit canopy. Hansen's crew were all Norwegians and had only a smattering of English; the pilot merely introduced them as 'his men' with a wave of the hand, producing a few friendly nods.

There was a wooden flight hut near the seaplane hangar. Hansen had brought some coffee from Alexandria and they drank it gratefully as they sat in the hut and waited for darkness. At last, Hansen glanced at his watched and announced that it was time to go.

The Heinkel had been brought down its slipway and now rode on the water that lapped the edge of Kalafrana Bay. The passengers stepped from the shingle onto one of the floats, then wormed their way into the bomb bay by means of a short ladder. The Norwegian crew saw that they were strapped in before entering the aircraft themselves, also using ladders which were then hauled aboard and stowed away.

A few minutes later the Heinkel was airborne, its twin BMW radial engines making a thunderous racket, after taxying out to its take-off point. The take-off itself had been surprisingly smooth, and the men in the bomb bay fervently hoped that the landing would match it. A tiny blue light had been fitted in the bay, so that its occupants were not in total darkness, but the roar of the engines made conversation impossible.

The thousand-mile flight to Alexandria took six and a quarter interminable hours, the Heinkel making a ground speed of about 160 miles per hour. In the bomb bay, Armstrong and the others dozed fitfully from time to time, only to be jolted awake as the aircraft ran through patches of turbulence. Once, an inspection hatch in the roof of the bomb bay slid back and the head and shoulders of the radio operator appeared; he handed down a flask of coffee and some sandwiches, which they shared. The second time he appeared, it was with the welcome news that they would soon be alighting.

The touchdown was accomplished with barely a jolt and a few minutes later, after taxying for some distance, the floatplane stopped and the pilot shut down the engines. Their ears ringing in the sudden, unaccustomed silence, the occupants of the bomb bay waited to see what would happen next. There was a splashing noise underneath the aircraft, the sound of voices, and then the bomb bay doors swung open, admitting daylight. Armstrong and the others, their seats bolted precariously on either side of the yawning gap, looked down and saw a naval rating grinning up at them.

"Right-oh, gentlemen, you can come down now. Watch your step, though. I'll give you a hand."

They undid their seat straps and swung down into the boat one by one, wincing a little with the ache of cramped limbs. Armstrong saw that the floatplane's crew were descending into a second boat, moored to a float on the other side of the aircraft. He saw, too, that the Heinkel was under cover in a kind of large boathouse, safe from the prying eyes of enemy reconnaissance aircraft.

The sailor started an outboard motor and steered the boat out of the shelter, into the dawn sun and the broad expanse of Alexandria Harbour. There were plenty of warships at home, and Dickie Baird kept up a running commentary as they cruised along, his face showing an almost childlike enthusiasm.

"Look, chaps, see those big battlewagons? That's the *Warspite*, *Barham* and *Valiant*. And the carrier there, that's the *Formidable*! She must have come up through the Red Sea."

There were cruisers and destroyers, too, and Armstrong had to admit that they made a splendid picture of naval might. It was on these ships, and on their sister vessels at Gibraltar, that Malta's survival depended.

The boat slid to a stop beside a metal ladder let into the side of a stone jetty, and the sailor indicated that his passengers were to disembark. Armstrong led the way, pulling himself up rung by rung, his kitbag over his shoulder, and hauled himself onto the jetty on his hands and knees.

He found himself staring at a pair of tan-coloured desert boots, topped by light-coloured tropical trousers that bore immaculate creases. Hurriedly scrambling to his feet, he looked hard at the figure that was silhouetted between him and the red ball of the rising sun.

"I've seen you make more dignified entrances, Armstrong," said Air Commodore Glendenning, a note of amusement in his voice. "Anyway, I'm glad you and your chaps made it all right. Let's go and have some breakfast, and afterwards I'll bring you up to date on the situation. Maybe we should make it an early afternoon briefing; I expect you could do with a bit of a rest after your journey."

Glendenning had arranged temporary accommodation for Armstrong and his party in a Royal Air Force Mess which, at the moment, was occupied by RAF personnel who had been hastily withdrawn from Greece and Crete and who were waiting to be reassigned to squadrons. After a welcome meal they slept for several hours, before being awakened by a mess orderly just in time for pre-lunch drinks. Bathed, shaved and refreshed, they congregated in the bar, where they got talking to some Hurricane pilots who had fought in the ill-starred Greek campaign.

"The main problem," said a deeply tanned flying officer, "was that we never had enough aircraft. We had five Hurricane squadrons, but we were never able to bring them up to full strength. Apart from that, when the front collapsed and things started moving quickly, we were shunted from one airstrip to another, and we never had time to get settled in before the Germans arrived and gave the place a pasting. It got to the point, at the end of April, where we hardly had any fighters left. We evacuated the last half dozen to Crete."

Armstrong had heard much talk about the defence of Crete, and whether the island might have been held. The flying officer shook his head in response to Armstrong's question.

"Not with fourteen fighters, sir, because that's all we had, including a few belonging to the Fleet Air Arm. At first, it wasn't too bad for us, because the Germans ignored the airfields and concentrated on attacking shipping in Suda Bay and on the approaches, so we were able to operate; our combat losses were made good by the two or three reinforcement Hurricanes that reached us daily from Egypt."

He set down his glass and lit a cigarette with hands which, Armstrong noticed, shook slightly.

"The problems really started to mount up when the Germans began hitting the airfields about the middle of May. The Fleet Air Arm chaps lost all three of their Fulmars and a couple of Gladiators in strafing attacks, so they attached themselves to us and carried on fighting. Within a couple of days we were down to four aircraft. Towards the end of May a dozen reinforcement Hurricanes were sent out from Egypt, but two of them were shot down by the bloody Navy as they approached the island and four more wrote themselves off on landing at Heraklion. We were lucky to get out, I can tell you."

Armstrong sympathised with the flying officer; he'd seen it all himself, in Norway and France. Too little, too late. Well, it would have to be a different story in North Africa, if Rommel's drive to Egypt was to be halted.

"Rommel," Air Commodore Glendenning pointed out a couple of hours later to Armstrong, "is quite a remarkable chap, by all accounts. And if we don't pin him down, we'll be in trouble."

The Air Commodore, Armstrong, Baird and Kalinski had assembled in a room that overlooked Alexandria's Eastern Harbour. The room itself was in some sort of administrative headquarters, and seemed to be occupied mostly by civilians. Armstrong did not ask what their role was, although the fact that armed guards were posted outside the main door suggested that it was not an unimportant one.

"In fact," Glendenning said, turning to a wall map, "Rommel would probably be in Cairo right now, if it were not for his preoccupation with this place here." His finger pointed to a spot on the coast.

"Tobruk. When the Axis forces made their dash into

Cyrenaica early in April, Rommel found himself flanked by our forces holding out here, representing a constant menace to his supply lines. So he divided his forces, leaving part to besiege Tobruk and the rest to push on and occupy the Halfaya Pass, the key to the eastward land route into Egypt. We managed to stop him there earlier this month, thanks to the timely arrival of a convoy which brought a couple of hundred tanks for the Western Desert Force, but he'll be on the offensive again before long, you may bank on it. He's already reached Sollum, and it's easy to see what his next objectives will be – Sidi Barrani, Matruh, El Alamein, Alexandria, and then Cairo. But he can't do it until he's at full strength, and he won't be at full strength until he's taken Tobruk. And there's another factor in our favour."

He paused, and they looked at him expectantly.

"Air power," Glendenning said. "According to our intelligence people, Rommel has about two hundred aircraft, and we outnumber him. Moreover, we expect the numbers to build up steadily. For example, the *Tiger* convoy – that's the one that brought the tanks – also brought forty-three Hurricanes, and more aircraft are being brought in via the African Reinforcement Route. Oh, I can see by your blank looks that you don't know what that is. Well, we've set up a trans-African ferry route, running from Takoradi on the Gold Coast via several staging points to its terminus in Egypt. The fighters – Hurricanes and Kittyhawks – are offloaded at Takoradi, assembled there, and flown along the route in batches of eight, led by a Blenheim whose crew does the navigation. The longest leg is six hundred and ninety miles, about three and a half hours' flying time. It's not much fun for the pilots; their cockpit canopies have to be painted white, or they'd get sunstroke. But it works, and we are gradually building up a reserve of aircraft at the maintenance units."

The Air Commodore gave one of his rare smiles. "We've got enough in reserve, in fact, to provide you with a squadron of Hurricanes, Armstrong. It's at Fayid, near the Great Bitter Lake south of Ismailia. We've assembled a pool of pilots there, too, so you can take your pick of them. I should warn you that they're a pretty bolshie lot, by all accounts, but they all have combat experience. I don't doubt that you can knock them into shape. You've got to have them ready within fourteen days, Armstrong. Your squadron must be combat-ready and deployed by then. Any questions?"

Armstrong looked at him. "Just one, sir. Exactly where are we being deployed?"

Glendenning looked a little embarrassed. "Oh, didn't I tell you? You will be responsible for the air defence of Tobruk. And as the nearest airstrip is a hundred and twenty miles away, that means you will be operating from inside the Tobruk perimeter."

Five

High in the sky over the Great Bitter Lake two Hurricanes danced in the sun, their Merlin engines wailing. In the leading aircraft Armstrong, the sweat drying on his face, was hurling his fighter around the sky in an effort to shake his pursuer off his tail.

He had to admit that the pilot of the other aircraft, Flight Sergeant Crosswell, an Australian, was very good. Twisting his neck to peer astern, he looked into the sun through his fingers. Crosswell's Hurricane was still there, a dark, indistinct shape poised in the glare half a mile away.

Armstrong smiled to himself and turned in the opposite direction, rocking his wings as though searching for the other aircraft. He glanced back again, squinting into the sun's rays, and saw a glitter as Crosswell turned after him. The other Hurricane closed rapidly in a shallow dive and Armstrong kept his eyes on it through his rear-view mirror, at the same time continuing to turn slightly this way and that.

Crosswell levelled out a few hundred yards astern. Armstrong, timing everything to perfection, suddenly opened the throttle and whipped his fighter round in a tight turn, thin contrails streaming from his wingtips. He kept the stick back in his stomach and the 'g' pushed him down into his seat as the Hurricane wheeled round on its wingtip. Crosswell, taken completely by surprise, overshot and Armstrong fastened himself on to the other's tail.

"Tacatacatacatac!" he shouted over the radio, imitating the noise of a machine-gun.

For the next three minutes Crosswell tried every trick in the book to shake off his pursuer, with no success at all. Armstrong stuck to him like glue, anticipating every move. At last, he decided to call it a day and pressed the R/T button.

"Blue One to Blue Two. Break off and return to base."

His voice was crisp and filled with authority, which was deliberate. He had no intention of according the Australian any familiarity – not, at least, until Crosswell learned how to behave himself. For Crosswell had a problem, and he didn't recognise it.

Armstrong was familiar with the Australian's record. From the combat point of view, it was impressive. He had worked his passage to England just before the outbreak of war and had joined the RAFVR; he had fought in France and in the Battle of Britain, shooting down a dozen enemy aircraft. But Crosswell's exploits had received no publicity; a mere sergeant pilot – as he then was – from the outback was not as newsworthy as a commissioned officer whose father, say, was a Member of Parliament. So Crosswell, who like most Australians was contemptuous of the British class system, had developed an unhealthy chip on his shoulder as a result, and somehow it had to be knocked off.

The two Hurricanes thundered low over Fayid, wingtip to wingtip, then pulled up sharply and broke into a tight circuit, curving down to land. They taxied in past a row of Curtiss P-40 Kittyhawks with sharks' teeth painted on their noses; the aircraft belonged to No 112 Squadron, which had lost all its Gloster Gladiators in Greece and which was in the process of rearming with the American fighter.

Armstrong had taken the opportunity to fly a Kittyhawk, and he had quickly formed an opinion of it. Its Allison engine performed well at low and medium altitudes, it had a formidable firepower of 6 point-five machine-guns, and a number of innovations such as electrically operated trim tabs. It also had the flying characteristics of a brick.

In short, the Kittyhawk was not an aircraft that could 'mix it' in a turning combat with an Me 109. It would, however, make an excellent fighter-bomber, and that was to be its main role in the new Desert Air Force that was slowly coming into being. Several South African and Australian squadrons were equipping with it.

The other Hurricanes came trickling back to Fayid in pairs over the next half hour. The training programme was now all but complete, with a couple of days still to go before the deadline imposed by Glendenning, and the pilots, despite their reputation, were fitting nicely into the team, with the possible exception of Crosswell. Armstrong studied them covertly as they clustered round the tea urn in the flight hut; it stood on a table under a whirling fan, its draught dissipating both the heat and the ever-present sandflies.

It was a cosmopolitan squadron, he thought, and no mistake. Of the ten pilots who currently made it up, only three were English; apart from himself, there were the two pilot officers, Billy Feather and Jackie Weston, now engaged in what appeared to be a heated argument. They would, Armstrong knew, be discussing tactics.

His eyes moved to another of the new pilots, Lieutenant Andreas Kostelas, a Greek, now in earnest conversation with Kalinski, the Pole. Kostelas had flown Gladiators in his native country and had a thorough knowledge of Italian air fighting tactics, which made him a very useful addition to the squadron.

That left Crosswell, the Australian, and his fellow flight sergeant, Don Petrie. The latter was a New Zealander of Scottish farming stock, and despite the fact that his family had emigrated to New Zealand in the middle of the nineteenth century he spoke with a determined Scots lilt. Armstrong was concerned by the apparent fact that the two NCO pilots did not like one another; he would have to keep an eye on that.

"You're looking thoughtful, Ken. Penny for 'em."

Armstrong looked round to see Dickie Baird at his elbow. He took a mouthful of tea, swallowed, and said: "Oh, I was just thinking that the squadron is becoming a bit like the league of nations. Three Englishmen, a Scot, an Irishman, a Pole, a South African, a Greek, an Aussie and a New Zealander. Dammit, we've got a Norwegian, too, haven't we? I almost forget about Hansen."

The Norwegian was still in Alexandria. Although

technically assigned to Armstrong's squadron, he had to remain on standby to carry out special operations, if such were dictated by GHQ in Cairo.

Baird grinned and nodded. "Yes, and don't forget there would have been one Englishman less, had it not been for a geographical accident of birth."

"What? Oh, yes, I see what you mean."

Armstrong was a native of Berwick-upon-Tweed, that much fought-over town that bestrode the border between England and Scotland. He had been born on the south side of the river, which made him a Northumbrian. If he had been born half a mile to the north, he would have been a Scot.

"Perish the thought," he added mildly. "Anyway, Dickie, changing the subject rapidly, I'm going to get off a signal to Air HQ this afternoon, telling them that we're combat-ready. We've done everything we can, and the chaps are champing at the bit. There's no point in hanging around here any longer. Tobruk it is, and the sooner the better."

He went over to the tea urn and refilled his mug. A calendar on the wall told him that it was the seventh of July. Idly, he wondered what was happening in the rest of the world, which just at the moment seemed pretty remote.

It was already seeming remote to *Capitano* Umberto Ricci, too, who was far from pleased with life. The order for his squadron to move to Libya had come right out of the blue; there had been no time to take a little leave, not even a few hours to say farewell to his family, his mother, father and sisters. Not to mention his girlfriends, all four of them.

61

His fighter group was now based at Derna. The town itself was right on the coast, which was not too bad; the airfield was a few kilometres inland, which was not too bad either. What upset Ricci was that the airfield was crowded with Germans, who appeared to have taken over the whole place, even though it was administered in theory by the *Regia Aeronautica*. Ricci did not like the Germans, who shaved every day instead of twice a week, like most sensible people.

Derna was only 160 kilometres from Tobruk; about twenty minutes' flying time, at economical cruising speed. Apart from Ricci's own 15th Squadron, Derna was home to a group of Ju 87 *Stukas* and a squadron of twin-engined Me 110s, and the newly-arrived Italians soon discovered that the Germans had appropriated all the best accommodation for themselves.

"We can only make the best of it," Ricci said philosophically when some of his pilots complained, "and pray that our stay here will be a short one."

Derna was also visited frequently by three-engined Junkers Ju 52 transports, bringing reinforcements for the motorised infantry element of the 15th *Panzer* Division that was besieging Tobruk. If Ricci had not disliked Germans so thoroughly, he would have felt sorry for them; their faces were a picture as they stepped from the aircraft. Where, they wondered, were the shady palm trees that formed the insignia of General Rommel's *Afrika Korps*? Here there were only flies, millions of them, rising in clouds that mingled with choking dust.

And when they reached Tobruk, they found themselves confronted by some of the finest fighting troops –

and certainly some of the best marksmen – in the world: the men of the 9th Australian Infantry Division. Blood-curdling tales were told about them – how, for instance, their patrols had an uncanny ability to appear out of nowhere in the night to descend silently on a single German or Italian strongpoint, throw their grenades and empty the magazines of their sub-machine guns into it before disappearing as swiftly and silently as they had arrived. They used Tommy guns, it was said, like the Chicago gangsters.

Fearsome tales were also told about the Tobruk anti-aircraft barrage. Although the last RAF fighters had been pulled out of the besieged garrison, the Royal Artillery – two regiments of 3.7-inch and captured Italian 102mm guns, plus three regiments with 40mm Bofors and the guns of ships in the harbour – made life for attacking aircrews very dangerous indeed.

"Attacks by dive-bombers have become so costly that they have almost ceased," an Italian intelligence officer, a *Tenente* called Martino, told Ricci. "The British have begun to unload their supplies by daylight, and as a result General Rommel has ordered the resumption of a maximum-effort air offensive. But here, let me brief you on the position."

In a few minutes, Martino gave Ricci a short resumé of the battle that had raged around Tobruk for the past two months. The first major Axis attack had begun on 30 April, after Rommel had tried to storm the perimeter defences in a precipitate rush, and failed. It had started with a continuous pounding by *Stukas* and artillery, against which the defenders' powers of retaliation were limited. They had engaged the attackers with anti-aircraft and small arms fire, and the British artillery had laid down counter-battery fire on the enemy gun positions, but ammunition had to be used sparingly; there would be no more supplies until the next moonless night, which was a week away.

As the dive-bombers flew away, the attacking infantry and tanks moved in against the western sector of the Tobruk perimeter. But the defenders were unbroken by the weight of explosives that had fallen on them, and the Germans and Italians encountered ferocious fire from the British artillery and tanks and the Australian infantry.

It was a grim and bitter battle, a battle of which Rommel wrote in a letter home:

"The Australians fought with remarkable tenacity. Even their wounded went on defending themselves with small arms fire, and stayed in the fight until their last breath. They were immensely big and powerful men, who without question represented an elite formation of the British Empire, a fact that was also evident in battle."

By the end of the first day the Axis forces had succeeded in penetrating the Tobruk defences and had established a two-mile salient into the Australian positions on the western sector of the perimeter. The salient included the important hill of Ras el Madaur, which dominated a large part of the defended area. For a week the battle raged unabated, the Germans throwing in fresh troops, but they were unable to advance further.

"However," Martino explained, "the Ras el Madaur salient remains a constant threat to the garrison. As you see from this map, the hard outer shell of the permanent defensive works has been breached, so that the opposing forces are facing each other from improvised foxholes. In essence, the defence of Tobruk now means the defence of this western sector. This is where most of the fighting has taken place. If the breakthrough comes, it will be here."

The intelligence officer scratched his bald head, on which a large fly had found a temporary resting place, and drew his thin lips into a smile.

"The foxholes do not provide very good cover," he said. "Quite a number of our men have been shot in the arse." He turned to a small table that bore several buff-coloured files and a tray on which stood a bottle of wine and some glasses. Opening one of the files, he leafed through its contents until he found a sheet of paper.

"A brief report," he said, handing it to Ricci, "prepared in an idle moment by one of our officers. It compares the attributes of our gallant German allies to those of our enemies."

Ricci looked at the closely-spaced lines of typescript. The report, he saw, pulled no punches. It stated:

'The Australians, who are the men our troops have had opposite them so far, are extraordinarily tough fighters. The German is more active in the attack, but the enemy stakes his life in the defence and fights to the last with extreme cunning. Our men, usually easy-going and unsuspecting, fall easily into his traps, especially as a result of their experiences in the closing stages of the European campaign.'

In which they got too accustomed to winning, Ricci thought, and read on.

'The Australian is unquestionably superior to the German soldier: 1. In the use of individual weapons, especially as snipers. 2. In the use of ground camouflage. 3. In his gift of observation, and the drawing of correct conclusions from his observation. 4. In using every means of taking us by surprise.

'Enemy snipers achieve astounding results. They shoot at anything they recognise. Several NCOs of the German battalion next to us have been shot through the head with the first bullet while making observations in the front line. Protruding sights in gun directors have been shot off, observation slits and loopholes have been fired on, and hit, as soon as they were seen to be in use (i.e. when the light background became dark). For this reason loopholes must be kept plugged with a wooden plug to be taken out only when they are used, so that they always show dark.'

"Have you seen Tobruk for yourself?" Ricci queried. Martino nodded, turning aside to pour a couple of glasses of wine. He handed one to the pilot, who sipped it appreciatively.

"Oh, yes, *Capitano*. I have flown around the Tobruk perimeter several times in an observation aircraft – taking care, of course, to select a pilot who did not want to be a hero! The whole town is surrounded by the debris of war; burned-out tanks, vehicles, everything. And Tobruk itself is a terrible sight; our bombers and artillery have flattened it. Only one house is still standing. A terrible sight. I have been there on the ground, too, and that is almost too fearsome to describe. The thirst!"

He drained the contents of his wine glass almost automatically and refilled it, offering the bottle to Ricci, who shook his head.

"You can scarcely imagine it," Martino went on. "If you touch a piece of bare metal, your hand is instantly burned. It is so hot that the soldiers fry eggs on the armour plating of their tanks. But it's the flies that make life really unbearable. They settle on the food in their thousands, and are certainly the cause of dysentery and other diseases among the men. That, and the fact that fresh fruit and vegetables are unknown in the front line. The Germans exist on sardines in oil and tinned sausages; we have our macaroni and tinned meat. I've got a tin here, as a matter of fact."

He picked a small round tin off the table. It was stamped with the letters 'AM'. Martino gave an unexpected grin.

"We issue this to the Germans, too. They consider it tough. In fact, I've heard it said that they think these initials stand for *Asinus Mussolini* – Mussolini's Ass."

Ricci laughed. "Speaking of animals," he said, "it looks as though we're going to need a wooden horse to get us into Tobruk, like the Greeks used to get into Troy."

Martino shrugged. "Maybe, *Capitano*. But don't forget one thing. They were camped outside the place for ten years before they managed it."

Six

Dawn, Friday, 11 July 1941: Tobruk

The Hurricanes arrived at Tobruk in pairs, with an interval of five minutes between each one, slanting down out of the north-eastern sky after making a detour out to sea. Armstrong had reasoned, quite rightly, that it would not do to have the whole squadron milling around over the town at once while the pilots waited their turn to land; the secret was to get down as quickly as possible, and get the aircraft under cover.

The squadron had spent the night at Sidi Barani, fifty miles inside Egypt at the eastern end of the Gulf of Sollum, a miserable, fly-blown place where air and ground crews lived in an extraordinary collection of shanties made from the hammered-out metal of cans, the wood of packing cases and scraps of canvas. Arabs occasionally wandered through the camp, looking for anything they could steal, staring in amazement at the sights that met their gaze, like tourists on holiday, doubtless wondering why the *ferengi* were too primitive to live in proper tents.

The Australians and South Africans at Sidi Barani were full of horror stories about what the extremes of climate did to their Kittyhawks. An engine, they said, might be expected to last for thirty hours' flying time or less before it became worn out, its cylinders pitted and its valves eroded by the scouring effect of the sand. Labouring liquid-cooled engines used vast quantities of oil and were prone to seize with little warning. Often, at night, the air was laden with a salty dampness that ate into everything with a relentless corrosive action. At the height of the day, aircraft tyres had to be covered with moist cloths to stop them bursting in the tremendous heat.

Sleep, the residents of Sidi Barani said, was impossible after five o'clock, when the first fly appeared. The fly would do a recce, go away, and reappear with twenty more. Within minutes there would be whole legions of the insects, savagely attacking any exposed part of the body. It would be much, much worse at Tobruk, a South African major told Armstrong cheerfully.

Well, Armstrong thought, as he throttled back and lowered the Hurricane's undercarriage, he would soon find out for himself. Praying that the anti-aircraft gunners had received the signal warning of the squadron's arrival, he looked ahead and picked out the airstrip without difficulty, lying on a plateau at the top of the Solaro escarpment, the saw-toothed range of hills that sloped down towards the town and harbour of Tobruk.

As he approached to land, followed by Crosswell and Petrie, Armstrong saw that the airstrip had been the object of a lot of attention from the opposition. There were bomb craters everywhere, with the shattered, burnt-out wrecks of aircraft scattered about the place. Not all, however, were British; he taxied in past the remains of an Italian Savoia bomber, a relic of the days when General O'Connor's forces had first captured the fortress.

He touched down without incident and a soldier waved him to a sandbagged emplacement with camouflage netting draped over it. The other Hurricanes were directed to similar revetments; all were safely down within fifteen minutes, their pilots stretching their legs as they climbed from their cockpits onto the wing, sliding down onto the baked rock and sand.

The pilots converged on their squadron commander, looking around them in curiosity. The airstrip was distinctly lacking in facilities; there were a few vehicles dotted here and there and a small stone building which turned out to be a sort of operations hut. A flight lieutenant wearing a cap that looked as though it had passed through a mangle several times emerged from it and approached Armstrong, saluting as he came.

"Good morning, sir," he said. "I'm Johnson. I've been on to our liaison bloke at HQ and there'll be a truck along to pick you up shortly. Do your aircraft need refuelling?"

Armstrong shook his head. "No, we topped up at Sidi Barani. Are you expecting trouble?"

Johnson looked thoughtfully at the western sky. "Could be," he said. "They've left us alone for a day or two. I think something's brewing."

Armstrong turned to Eamonn O'Day, who had been evesdropping, and told him to form a battle flight, just in case. O'Day picked the two Englishmen, Feather and Weston, who looked pleased and wandered off with the Irishman to seek some shade in the stone hut, where some tea was on the brew. While the others waited for the promised truck, Armstrong quizzed Johnson about conditions in Tobruk. The RAF officer tilted back his cap.

"Well," he said, "I've been here since the start of the siege, and nothing's improved. I came in with No 6 Squadron, which is Middle East Command's Army Co-operation outfit. We had Lysanders at first, but our 'A' Flight had just re-equipped with tactical recce Hurricanes and was at Agedabia, flying recce sorties over Tripolitania, when Rommel started his offensive. We pulled out pretty sharpish and moved back to Tobruk; by this time 'B' Flight had also received Hurricanes and No 73 Squadron had moved in to take over air defence. Since we were primarily an artillery co-operation unit, we were kept pretty busy, especially after the Huns moved a squadron of Me 109s up to El Adem."

Armstrong pricked up his ears at that. "I didn't know there were any 109s in North Africa," he said. "According to the intelligence reports I've seen, the only German fighters around here are 110s."

"That's quite true at the moment," Johnson told him, "But the 109s were here a few weeks ago, all right. And they were 109Fs, the latest model. They took us by surprise, I can tell you. We'd been having a fair old ball with the *Stukas* until then, and suddenly there were 109s everywhere. They made a habit of catching the Hurricanes and Lysanders as they were landing. Poor old 73 Squadron took a terrible beating and had to be pulled out, and within a week or two we were down to our last serviceable aircraft, too."

He looked suddenly puzzled. "You're right, though.

We haven't seen any 109s for a while. Just 110s, *Stukas* and the Italians, of course. Maybe they've sent them off to Russia, or something."

In fact, although the RAF pilots had no way of knowing it, the sudden disappearance of the Me 109F was the consequence of a technical problem. The German fighter had only been in operational service for a few weeks when the complete tail assembly broke off one, resulting in the loss of the aircraft and its pilot. Tests showed that the tail section had an unexpected structural weakness, and all aircraft in service were withdrawn for modifications.

After a while, a battered, pock-marked Fiat five-ton truck came crawling up the escarpment. The driver was a lean, sunburned Australian with a considerable growth of bristle on his face, out of which a limp cigarette end protruded. His dress consisted of a torn slouch hat, a pair of filthy shorts and boots that were scoured white by the sand. He dropped off a bag of supplies, said "Yer comin', or not?" to the group of newly arrived pilots, and climbed back into the cab.

The drive down the escarpment was a nerve-racking experience. The Australian kept his foot hard down on the floorboards for most of the way and maintained the pace, sounding his horn furiously, through the shattered streets of Tobruk itself. White-faced, the passengers clung to the nearest immovable object with sweating hands and breathed a collective sigh of relief when the truck eventually screeched to a halt in front of a white concrete building that stood on the high ground on the northern side of the harbour. The driver lit another cigarette and indicated the building with his thumb.

"Navy House," he said. "Everybody fresh in reports to the communications room. Through the main door, down the corridor, turn left and down the steps. Second door on the left. Anyone for the canteen?"

Armstrong told Baird and Kalinski, his two flight commanders, to accompany him, leaving the others to the mercy of the Australian driver and ordering them to report back to the airstrip by noon. As Armstrong and his companions entered Navy House, the nerve centre of Tobruk's defences, they soon found that security was excellent; they had to identify themselves three times to armed military policemen before finally being admitted to the communications room.

They stepped inside, gazing around them with interest. A bank of signals equipment stood along one wall; maps covered the other three walls, and more maps were spread over a low table that stood in the centre of the room. Electric lights provided the only source of illumination, for the room was underground.

An Australian Army major, who had been poring over the maps on the table with a couple of other officers, straightened up and came over to the newcomers, extending a hand. Armstrong took it, introducing himself and his flight commanders. The Australian, whose name was Brady, told an orderly to organise some tea and indicated the map.

"Come and take a look at the situation," he said. "How much do you know?"

Armstrong was forced to admit that he knew very little.

'Right, then," Brady said, "let's take it from the beginning. When Ninth Div got back to Tobruk from El

Agheila in March, we set about strengthening the old Italian perimeter, which was pretty much run down." His finger traced a semicircle on the map, some ten miles from the town.

"This," he continued, "is known as the Red Line." He moved his finger. "Two miles behind it we built the Blue Line, which is really a continuous minefield covered by barbed wire and strong points housing anti-tank and machine-guns. There are an awful lot of mines between the Red and Blue lines, so if you have to bale out I don't recommend coming down there!"

Brady tapped the south-west corner of the perimeter with his index finger. "So far, this is the sector against which the enemy has launched his strongest attacks. Further along the perimeter it's mostly open desert, with little cover for tanks and infantry, and at the other end there are some wadis – dried-up river beds – which make it pretty impossible terrain for armour. So we reckon Jerry will keep up the pressure against the south-west corner, but we can never be sure. If you chaps can manage the odd recce flight, it'll be a godsend. We haven't had any real air recce since the Lysanders got clobbered; since then we've had to rely on aircraft from Sidi Barani and Matruh, and by the time their information gets to us the tactical situation can have changed completely. What we need is someone who can take off at a few minutes' notice, have a quick look at what's going on over the other side, and radio the gen back to us so that the defences can act accordingly."

After an hour and a half, Armstrong and the others felt they knew all there was to know about the defence of

Tobruk, thanks to the detailed picture built up by Brady. The Australian also spoke of the part played so far by the 9th Australian Infantry Division in the desert war, and spoke with the utmost admiration of the divisional commander, Major General Leslie Morshead, who now commanded the garrison at Tobruk.

Nicknamed 'Ming the Merciless' by the rank and file, Morshead was an austere and highly capable officer who had once been a schoolmaster before serving in the Great War, when he had taken part in the costly and tragic Gallipoli landings and later commanded a battalion in France. Between the wars he had returned to civilian life, as a branch manager of the Sydney offices of the Orient Line, but had continued to soldier in his spare time. His powers of leadership had been very much in evidence during the demoralising retreat from El Agheila; and with the 9th Division in relative safety behind the Tobruk perimeter, he had told his men in no uncertain terms that there would be no more running. Tobruk was a fortress from which the Commonwealth forces would sally forth to hit the enemy, and hit him hard.

They had lunch in Navy House – tinned meat and reconstituted mashed potatoes, that tasteless concoction known as POM – which had led to the Australians bestowing the nickname 'Pommies' on their English comrades-in-arms – followed by tinned rice pudding. There was not a serious shortage of food – not yet, anyway, although the diet was monotonous and unhealthy – but there was a shortage of water. Each man was rationed to half a gallon a day, and by itself the water, which was very salty, was barely palatable.

After lunch, Brady glanced at his watch. It was twelve-thirty.

"Time for you to have a quick look around," the Australian said. "There won't be an air raid before two o'clock; for some reason there never is. You can set your clock by the bastards. They come just after dawn, or after two. The truck will pick you up outside in an hour."

They inspected Tobruk harbour, which was a shambles. They gazed at it in astonishment, wondering how any vessel could offload stores. Burnt-out, rusting ships lay all around the fringes; others, half submerged, poked funnels like accusing fingers from the oily water, or raised their long, dark undersides towards the sky like prehistoric sea monsters struggling for a glimpse of the sun. Every cove and bay around the harbour seemed full of floating wreckage, each island of debris surrounded by its own halo of scum and oil. Wherever the three men looked a scene of utter devastation met their eyes; on land, the once neat white houses lay pulverised and shattered, torn apart successively by the heavy shells of the Royal Navy's warships in the days when Tobruk was an Italian garrison, and more recently by the bombs of the *Luftwaffe* and the *Regia Aeronautica*.

Even the men swarming over the quay, where a ship was unloading, looked like ragged, emaciated scarecrows moving through some infernal ruin. They were a mixed bunch of Australian, British and Indian soldiers, a few sailors and some native Libyans, all covered in a uniform coating of yellow-grey dust. Armstrong wrinkled his nose as a strange, pungent stench assailed his nostrils; a smell whose main ingredients seemed to be burnt cordite, crude oil, sewers and human sweat. Baird, used to the atmosphere of North African seaports, saw his expression and grinned. "Don't worry," he said. "You'll get accustomed to it."

They picked their way along the north-east side of the harbour, skirting bomb craters, mounds of tumbled masonry and piles of empty crates and drums. There were several gun pits in the vicinity, solidly built and well protected, with stone and concrete foundations surrounded by a wall of 40–gallon oil drums filled with sand and stones. On top of the drums was a parapet of sandbags, many of them filled with old Italian flour, which became as hard as cement when mixed with sea water. The gun crews were mostly relaxing, lying on iron bedsteads – also former property of the Italians – beneath their camouflage netting.

In the distance, gunfire rolled across the desert beyond the escarpment.

"Some poor beggars on the perimeter catching it again." The speaker was a gunner subaltern, who was perched on top of some sandbags reading a letter from home. It'll be our turn again shortly, no doubt. I just hope the lads get the unloading finished on time. It's mostly ammunition they're bringing in, and we can do with it." He looked back towards the quay, where the men were working like an army of ants under the direction of a portly, sweating lieutenant.

"I suppose there's a mad rush for the shelter when the alert goes up," Armstrong said. The subaltern laughed.

"Not a bit of it. Nobody stops work or makes for the shelter – which, by the way, is that big cave you can see over there – until a red flag is flown from Navy House. As long as our chaps go on working the natives will more or less stand firm, but once the flag appears you'll see the most impressive 150-yard mass sprint imaginable. The trouble is, when the blokes get to the cave, which runs about sixty feet underground, the first lot tend to cluster in the entrance to get a grandstand view of what's going on, so you usually get a big, struggling mass of sweaty humanity milling around outside, all trying to get in. It's bloody crazy. They're going to get a bomb on top of them one of these days. Personally, I'd rather take my chance in the open."

"Well," said the keen-eyed Kalinski, "you won't have to wait for long. Here they come. We've been caught short, Ken."

"Christ, they're early!" the gunner gasped, thrusting his letter into the pocket of his shorts and looking up into the western sky, where a cluster of black dots had become visible. They could hear the drone of aero-engines now, and the sound sent shivers down their spines. Even at this distance, there was no mistaking the throbbing beat of the *Stuka*.

All around, the crews of the anti-aircraft guns were jumping to action stations. Armstrong glanced towards Navy House; the red flag was still not showing, and the men on the quay went on working, although some of them were glancing apprehensively at the sky.

"Better get under cover," Armstrong said tersely. "We've no chance of making it back to the airstrip. Remember, it doesn't look good to run, and anyway it will be a couple of minutes before they're overhead."

At that moment, with a terrific crash, a stick of bombs erupted across the harbour, turning several small boats into matchwood and raising great fountains of oily water. The three men ducked instinctively as fragments of wood whistled overhead. The next instant, the anti-aircraft battery nearest to them opened up with a fearful banging.

Armstrong looked up, craning his neck. High above Tobruk, four aircraft cruised in immaculate formation. Even as he watched, more bombs exploded around the harbour, raising a pall of dust and smoke and shaking the ground with their concussion. Fortunately, none fell near the ship that was still being unloaded.

At last, the red flag was unfurled above Navy House.

"Did you say something about taking cover?" Baird yelled. In unison, they dived headlong into the nearest gun pit. A gunner pushed them against the wall of oil drums. "Just keep out of the bloody way, that's all!" he shouted.

The four bombers had turned and were flying off towards the west, still in perfect formation. Yet again, the Italians had demonstrated their skill in high-level precision bombing.

"Crafty bastards," Baird said, shouting to make himself heard above the din. "Their game is to keep the guns occupied and give the dive-bombers a chance. Look!"

The *Stuka* formation was turning towards the south, the Germans' intention clearly being to dive on the fortress out of the sun. They were carefully keeping out of range until the last moment. In the meantime, two more formations of Italian bombers came swinging in over the coast, like silvery fish in the brilliant sunlight, and the Tobruk anti-aircraft barrage turned its full fury on them. The air rang with the clang of metal as the gunners slammed home the long shells. The barrels turned menacingly in response to shouted orders as the predictors pinpointed the altitude of the incoming bombers.

Close by Navy House, on the high ground, there was a sandbagged emplacement surrounded by a battery of loud-speakers. From this excellent vantage point, commanding a view of the whole harbour, a gunnery officer controlled the Tobruk barrage. Now, above the drone of engines and the hundred other sounds, his voice rang out clearly.

"Tobruk – engage!"

With a massive, skull-splitting crash, every gun around the harbour sent its shells blasting towards the enemy in a single salvo. Dazed by the noise, their ears ringing, Armstrong and his companions kept their eyes on the Italian formation. After a delay that seemed endless, the small white puffs of the shell bursts spattered the sky around the bombers.

The Italians cruised serenely on. Seconds later, Armstrong heard the howl of their bombs and flung himself face down alongside the others an instant before the first stick exploded a bare hundred yards away with a series of terrific bangs, pulverising a cluster of already badly damaged buildings near the quay. The pilots, who did not have steel helmets, covered their heads as best they could as stones and debris showered the area like hail, accompanied by clouds of choking, swirling dust. More bombs fell in the vicinity of the harbour and in the town itself, choking the streets with more rubble. Pillars of smoke boiled upwards, brown and evil, dragging dust and powdered cement into their vortices until the sun shone pale and murkily through an opaque veil.

The anti-aircraft guns fired another salvo, and once more the Italian bombers were boxed in by the smoke of the bursts. Again they cruised on, apparently untouched. Then, suddenly, a cheer went up from the gunners as one of the bombers began to trail a slender, almost imperceptible thread of smoke. The trail became thicker and the bomber turned, losing height and dropping out of formation. White flames burst from ruptured fuel tanks and its dive became steeper until it was plunging vertically, the smoke of its fall marking the sky like a dark crayon-line. It fell several miles away, up the coast. Parachutes, two tiny white dots against the blue, broke away and drifted slowly out to sea.

There was no time for jubilation. Armstrong burrowed deeper against the protective wall of the gun pit as the rending screech of a diving *Stuka* assailed his senses. Like great, malignant birds of prey the gull-winged dive-bombers came howling down over the harbour, braving a barrage of Bofors shells that swept the sky up to 3,000 feet. The guns, magnificently co-ordinated, traversed the area above the harbour in regular patterns, scattering chains of fire in the path of the enemy aircraft.

It seemed incredible that anything could survive such an inferno, yet the *Stukas* screamed down through the ack-ack bursts in line astern unharmed and pulled out of their dives, the black, sinister eggs of their bombs curving down to explode among the gun emplacements. Armstrong's breath was knocked from his body as the earth heaved under him. The crash of successive bomb bursts blotted out everything, blinding and suffocating. It seemed as though the whole world were dissolving in tortured darkness. He clasped his hands over his ears, willing the nightmare to go away, but it went on without end, until every nerve in his body screamed at him to run, to jump to his feet and risk the sleet of steel, to fill his lungs with air again, even though death might follow in the next instant.

This was worse than anything Armstrong had experienced in Norway or France. This was Tobruk, in the summer of 1941.

Suddenly, there was silence. Armstrong and his companions got to their feet groggily, white-faced. They were surrounded by empty shell cases. One of the gunners offered Armstrong a cigarette and he took it gratefully, drawing hard on it in a bid to calm his nerves. Baird and the normally unflappable Kalinski were equally as shaken.

"I wonder what happened to the Battle Flight?" Baird said. His voice sounded flat and tinny.

"Not enough warning, I guess," Armstrong said. "Put yourself in O'Day's place. He'd have realised that he hadn't a hope in hell of gaining altitude and getting into position for an attack before the bombers were over their target. If he and the others had taken off, all they'd have done would be to advertise the fact that we're here. The enemy will know that soon enough. We won't be caught with our pants down again."

He looked towards Navy House. Already someone had hauled down the red flag, and work on unloading the freighter, which had escaped undamaged apart from a few splinter scars, continued almost as though nothing had happened. For the first time, Armstrong sensed the immense spirit that pervaded the Tobruk garrison, a determination not to be beaten, no matter what the cost. Suddenly, he felt enormously gratified to be there, to be part of this supreme defiance.

Seven

Sunday, 13 July 1941: Tobruk

P ilot Officer Billy Feather looked up at the Western sky
and drummed his fingertips impatiently on the fabric
of his Hurricane's wings. The waiting was beginning to
get him down. There had been several false alarms that
morning, and after each one the knot in his stomach had
got that little bit tighter. His shirt was already soaked
with sweat under his Mae West lifejacket. The rest of
his clothing consisted of shorts, socks and desert boots;
although it would be bitterly cold at high altitude, to wear
heavier clothing while on readiness was to risk almost
certain heat-stroke.

He glanced over at the wing commander, sitting uncon-
cernedly on an upturned wooden crate near his aircraft's
blast pen, leafing through a tattered magazine. He knew
that Wing Commander Armstrong was a veteran of three
campaigns – Norway, France and the Battle of Britain
– and was gratified to be serving under an officer of
such experience. He had felt a glow of satisfaction that
morning, when Armstrong had selected him to fly as his
number two. The South African, van Berg, would be

flying in the number three position, with Feather's friend Weston as number four.

Gone were the days when RAF fighters flew in tight battle formations. They had now taken a leaf out of the Germans' book and flew in sections of four, widely spaced, each pilot covering his neighbour.

Suddenly, there was a commotion. Flight Lieutenant Johnson came running out of the operations hut, brandishing a Very pistol. There was a crack and a white flare arced up into the heat haze that danced and shimmered over the airstrip. Almost before he realised what he was doing, Feather had grabbed his helmet from where it had been lying on the Hurricane's wing and was pulling it on as he stepped into the cockpit and settled down on the parachute pack. He strapped himself in quickly, helped by one of the RAF ground crew who had been ferried into Tobruk a couple of days earlier.

The Hurricane's Merlin engine choked a couple of times, then started with a bang. Long flames shot briefly from its exhausts. Feather reached up and slammed the hood closed; furnace-like though the cockpit interior was, to taxi with the hood open was to risk being half choked to death by clouds of swirling dust. One of the airmen had jumped up onto the wing root and was hanging on with one hand, battered by the slipstream from the propeller, grinning and waving. Feather realised that he was wishing him good luck and gave him a thumbs-up; the airman dropped out of sight.

Feather released the brakes, opened the throttle a little and took the Hurricane out of its blast pen onto the rough track that converged, with others like it, onto the path of beaten sand and crushed rock that served as the runway. Over on the left the wing commander's fighter was also moving forward, dragging the inevitable cloud of dust in its wake. More dust, billowing up from various points around the field, betrayed the whereabouts of other taxying Hurricanes.

He swung into position behind and to the right of Armstrong, swinging the Hurricane's nose from side to side to ensure that there were no obstacles in his path. Armstrong's fighter was a grey ghost in its shroud of dust. Recalling his unpleasant experiences in the Greek campaign, Feather gave a quick glance over his shoulder. This was the dangerous time, the time when enemy fighters might come streaking down, shark-like, to strafe and destroy.

The sky astern was clear. The only aircraft immediately behind were the Hurricanes manned by van Berg and Weston. Feather eased open the throttle, matching his speed to that of Armstrong's aircraft as he began his take-off roll. Ahead of him, the wing commander's Hurricane, its tail up, bounced a couple of times and then lifted into the air. Feather's own aircraft hit a patch of uneven surface and lurched viuolently as its tail also rose; Feather worked the rudder pedals frantically, striving to keep the aircraft straight, and eased back the stick. The rumble of the undercarriage ceased as the fighter became airborne; Feather kept the nose down for a few seconds, building up speed, then pulled up sharply after Armstrong, who was turning steeply to the right, climbing hard.

The Hurricanes continued to turn, gaining altitude as they passed over Tobruk harbour. It was crowned by a layer of bronze haze, and beneath it, spreading like some foul poison, was a carpet of some strange grey-green substance. Feather realised that he was looking at a smokescreen, put up by the harbour defences.

Armstrong's fighter was two hundred yards ahead and well over to the left. Astern, van Berg and Weston were closing fast, also out on the left, dropping into their number three and four positions. They were over the sea now, still climbing and passing 8,000 feet; Feather realised that Armstrong was leading the formation out to sea as it climbed to avoid the enemy anti-aircraft guns on the perimeter, the deadly 88-millimetre weapons that were devastating against both aircraft and tanks. So far, the wing commander had kept radio silence. As far as it was known, the Germans and Italians were unaware that RAF fighters had returned to Tobruk. With luck, they would come as a nasty surprise.

Automatically, Feather checked his instruments, keeping an eye on engine temperatures and pressures. He lowered his seat, which had been raised for take-off to give maximum forward visibility, so that it was now below the level of the armour plating behind him. He found that he was trembling slightly, and willed himself to relax.

The Hurricanes burst out of a layer of haze at 10,000 feet and went on climbing. Feather turned his oxygen fully on and looked around. The African coast was a white strip, two miles below. Sea and sky merged into a single cerulean backdrop; it was like flying inside a luminous blue ball and the light was painful to the eyes, even through tinted goggles. Far off to the north, 180 miles away, lay the scene of Feather's last battle, the island of Crete. He had been lucky to get away, very lucky indeed. Everything else was a bonus, after the hell of Crete.

Fourteen thousand feet, and there was still no sign of the enemy. The Hurricane pilots did not have the benefit of a radar-controlled interception; the only clue that enemy bombers were inbound had come from the small RAF wireless monitoring section in Navy House, its job to detect radio transmissions that indicated a raiding force was assembling over the enemy airfields. Fortunately, neither the Germans nor the Italians were particularly security conscious when it came to radio telephony chatter; there was usually plenty of it.

Search the sky, Feather told himself. Search the sky, and live. It's the one you don't see who will get you. The roar of the engine became part of his senses. He was enclosed in a strange, unreal silence. Watch it, his brain screamed, don't drift. At 16,000 feet the fighter formation levelled out and followed Armstrong as the wing commander began a gentle turn back towards the coast. A thin stream of air was whistling into Feather's cockpit through some unidentified chink, freezing his bare arms. It was cold now, and his sweaty shirt felt as stiff as cardboard.

Where the hell were they? Searching, searching above, across and behind, forcing his eyeballs to relax. Don't strain, he thought, you see nothing that way. The sun was a great white ball of icy light that seared the eyes but did not warm the flesh.

Catfish Red One was calling, his voice garbled and

distorted. Feather could make out only Kalinski's callsign. Then the radio cleared, and there was no mistaking the urgency in the Polish pilot's message.

"Bogies, four o'clock high!"

Bogies – that meant the aircraft were not yet positively identified as enemies, or 'bandits'. Feather craned his neck, fighting the constriction of his seat harness to peer over his right shoulder. He could see nothing. Where, for Jesus' sake, where were they?

Then he saw them, a shoal of dark crosses, curving round behind the Hurricanes from the right, coming round to seven o'clock and turning in. The Hurricanes, still level and turning, were now heading back towards Tobruk, with the sun high to the right.

Armstrong's voice sounded over the R/T. "OK, I've got them. Macchis, I think. Let's see if we can suck 'em in."

The Italian fighters were shadowing them, keeping pace. There was still no sign of any bombers; the fighters must have been sent in first to clear the area. Previous raids had been unescorted, so the enemy must have got wind of the Hurricanes' presence at Tobruk.

"Look out, here they come. Wait for it."

Armstrong's voice was calm and unruffled. The Hurricanes went on turning and the Macchis turned with them, levelling out and arrowing in from astern, using the speed they had built up in their dive to overhaul the British fighters. Feather counted ten of them, so the odds were even. His hands were sweaty and slippery on the stick. The leading Macchis were growing larger in one corner of his rear-view mirror. God, would Armstrong never order them to break? The enemy fighters were close, far too close! If the break didn't come in another second he was going to do it anyway, and to hell with the consequences . . .

"Break left!"

They stood the Hurricanes on their wingtips, hauling control columns back into their stomachs. The fighters came round in a turn that crushed the pilots down in their seats, dragging down the flesh of their cheeks. Feather's mouth sagged open with the brute force of it and he felt suddenly sick. Three Macchi 200s flashed overhead, their tracers punching holes in thin air, and Armstrong reversed his turn, leading the other three fighters of his flight in pursuit. Feather clung to Armstrong's gyrating Hurricane in desperation, covering the leader's tail, and saw Armstrong open fire, still in the turn, his bullets finding their mark in a Macchi which suddenly belched white smoke, toppled over and went down vertically. Then Armstrong reversed his turn yet again, facing the other Macchis, and once more a great fist rammed Feather's body down, punching the air from his struggling lungs.

A Macchi shot across his nose and he fired, hopelessly, for the deflection angle was impossible, and almost cried out aloud when the enemy fighter's tail disintegrated. The Macchi flicked away below and he saw no more of it; he would only be able to claim a 'damaged'.

He glanced round, and miraculously the Italian fighters had vanished, for the moment at least. All four Hurricanes of the leading flight were still with one another, joining up into their section formation as Armstrong curved out of his turn into level flight. Feather had the oddest sensation of no longer being master of his own fate. All he knew was that he had to cling to Armstrong's Hurricane like a leech, making sure that nothing pounced on it, alternately watching its manoeuvres and tearing his eyes away from it to search the sky, hoping to God that van Berg and Weston were doing their job and guarding the section's blind spots.

"Bandits five o'clock, high!"

"Bandits three o'clock, level!"

Oh Christ, it was the nightmare of Greece and Crete all over again. Which way to turn? Which way? Then, once again, Armstrong's calm voice, restoring a measure of sanity, its very tones encouraging them to relax and keep their wits about them.

"Wait for it, chaps. The high ones are ours. Wait for the break!"

He was coolly telling them to ignore the Macchis boring in from three o'clock, and to concentrate on the ones astern. Then Feather suddenly knew why. Climbing hard under the Macchis over on the right were the four Hurricanes of Dickie Baird's Blue Flight. Feather hadn't noticed them at all until this moment, and it didn't look as though the Italians had spotted them either.

The Macchis astern were diving now, positioning themselves to get on the tails of Armstrong's four Hurricanes, and Feather marvelled that the Italians seemed to fall for the old trick every time.

"Break right!"

Once more the frantic merry-go-round, the desert gyrating under the wings, the heavy, clutching hand of gravitational force as the Hurricanes swung round to face

91

the attackers. The Macchis came in like sharks, fleeting and deadly, growing in size with terrifying speed. There were six of them, and as the four Hurricanes swung out of their turn the Italians split into two groups of three, skidding away to left and right. Feather's mind registered their curious but effective desert camouflage scheme, yellow ochre with dark red and green blotches splashed across it, the large white crosses standing out starkly on their tail fins.

The Hurricanes split up too, van Berg and Weston chasing one group of Macchis while Armstrong and Feather went after the others. Suddenly, Armstrong's voice crackled urgently over the radio.

"All Catfish aircraft from Catfish leader. Leave the fighters! *Stukas* nine o'clock, low. Let's go!"

Armstrong's Hurricane rolled over on its back and disappeared under Feather's port wing. Feather rolled too, feeling his seat harness bite into his shoulders as he pulled through, half-rolling again as the Hurricane's nose went down into a vertical dive, looking ahead for his leader and the enemy dive-bombers. He located Armstrong's fighter immediately, and a split second later sighted the target: a formation of about twenty Junkers 87s, flying at 12,000 feet in three broad arrowheads.

Another glance back as he levelled out, a few hundred yards behind Armstrong, curving round for a beam attack on the leading formation of bombers: the Macchis were still pouring down, gaining ground all the time.

To hell with it! Ahead of him, Armstrong was already opening fire, grey smoke trails streaming back from his wings. Feather selected a Junkers which was flying at a slightly lower altitude than the others and pushed the stick forward a little, converging on it, firing as it leaped towards him. The *Stukas* belonged to a German unit, a fact betrayed by the black crosses and swastikas emblazoned on their sandy camouflage.

The Hurricane shuddered with the recoil of its guns and the *Stuka* went into a sudden climbing turn. He fired again as the gunsight framed the bomber's nose and engine, seeing the long glasshouse cockpit shatter into a thousand flying slivers as his bullets traversed its length. The Junkers' wings loomed large in front of him as he loosed off a deflection shot inside its turn, glimpsing a vivid flash and a puff of smoke from the engine before his target whirled away and vanished.

Orange golf balls were flashing past his cockpit, just above his starboard wing, making a strange crackling noise that was clearly audible above the roar of the engine. He stared at them, mesmerised, for a fraction of a second that stretched into infinity, then tore his eyes away and rammed the stick forward and to the left, diving away and looking back at the same time.

A hundred yards behind him was the head-on silhouette of another Ju 87, its pilot blazing away at him with the 7.9mm machine-guns mounted in his wings. The Hurricane lurched and he felt, rather than heard, a series of bangs somewhere behind the armour plating of his seat. He tightened the turn to the left, coming out of the dive and pulling up steeply, keeping the Junkers in sight all the time as it shot past. At the top of his climb he winged over, curving down to get on the bomber's tail.

He gave a quick glance around to check that he was

in no immediate danger, then went after the Ju 87 at full boost. The Junkers, its wings heavy with fat bombs and its dive brakes fully open, was nosing down through 8,000 feet, and Feather realised with a start that the fight had taken him practically over the outskirts of Tobruk. Ahead, and becoming more dangerously close with every second, a thundercloud of shell bursts filled the sky over the harbour.

Feather overhauled the bomber quickly, ignoring the fireballs that flitted towards him from the rear gun position. The tail unit and part of the rear fuselage crept into his sight. He made a small correction and the luminous dot of the sight moved a few degrees to the left, centring on the *Stuka*'s port wing root. The rear gunner was still firing, and Feather felt two more thumps as bullets struck the Hurricane. There was no time to worry about that now. The range was down to seventy-five yards and the bomber's dive was growing steeper. Feather stuck to it grimly and jabbed his thumb down on the firing button.

His aim was good. There was a burst of white smoke and great chunks broke away from the wing root, whirling back in the slipstream. A fuel tank in the wing exploded and a river of fire streamed past the bomber's tailplane. Feather gave a touch of right rudder and saw his bullets punch into the Junkers' fuselage.

The *Stuka* was finished. Feather throttled back to avoid colliding with the blazing mass, then turned away sharply as the rear gunner, incredibly, opened fire once more. He had time only for one short burst, however, before the *Stuka* heeled over and plunged earthwards, spewing blazing debris as it fell. It exploded a few thousand feet lower down in a soundless gush of smoke and flame. There had been no parachutes and Feather felt sorry for the German gunner. The man had shown plenty of guts; he had deserved to live.

Feather brought the Hurricane round in a tight turn, aware of the dangers of flying straight and level for more than a few seconds and looking round to get his bearings. The fight had carried him back to the west of Tobruk, thankfully clear of the barrage. He could see no other aircraft in the vicinity.

His fuel was running low and he decided to head for the airstrip, hoping that it had not been bombed. Feeling very alone and exposed, he turned east, and in that same heart-stopping flash of time he saw the Macchis.

There were two of them, streaking up from the south-west, their aggressive head-on silhouettes already twinkling with the flashes of their guns as they curved in towards the lone Hurricane. Instinctively Feather turned towards them, catching a hazy impression of a third as it came at him from a different angle. He looked again for the first two but they had already vanished, their high speed carrying them a long way past after missing him with their first firing pass, but now two more were coming in from the right, cutting inside his turn.

Feather's hands on the stick were slippery and wet and sweat poured into his eyes, half blinding him. At all costs he had to keep turning; it was his only hope of salvation. With his radio dead there was no possibility of calling for help. He would have to sort out this predicament all by himself.

A Macchi flashed under his nose, appearing ahead of

him and entering his sight for a fraction of a second. He loosed of a rapid burst and the Italian flicked away sharply. The two on his right were turning with him, aiming to cut him off, closing in for the kill. His arms ached with the effort of hauling on the stick, for the Hurricane's control surfaces were stiffened by the speed of the combat. Feather knew that he wasn't turning tightly enough and increased the pressure, bringing the stick back into his stomach with the wings almost vertical, attempting the impossible.

The Hurricane protested, like a thoroughbred being forced at an unmanageable fence. A great tremble ran through her, and the next instant the desert was rotating above Feather's head as she stalled out of the turn and went into a spin. Frantically, for he was now very low, Feather applied full rudder in the opposite direction to that of the spin's rotation and pushed the stick forward. The Hurricane responded beautifully and pulled out into a shallow dive, levelling out a mere hundred feet above the desert.

Rocks, sand and scrub flashed beneath the fighter's wings. Feather had no idea of his position. A quick look up and behind revealed two Macchis a few thousand feet above him, waggling their wings; they seemed to have lost him, but they were still with him, flying on the same heading and keeping pace. He realised that he must be in their blind spot, but that situation could be only temporary; they were bound to spot him soon.

Now he was faced with another problem: the needles of his oil pressure and temperature gauges were almost off the clock. A few moments later, Feather's worst fears were confirmed when smoke began to stream from under the engine cowling, and his ears detected a new, ominous note in the sound of the Merlin.

The smoke became denser, obscuring his forward vision. He could hardly see a thing. He waggled his wings, looking for an open space. The engine sounded like two skeletons making love on a tin roof. Suddenly, it seized altogether with a terrific crunch. Hurriedly, the pilot reached up and slid back the cockpit canopy.

The smoke died away, and suddenly Feather could see again. He spotted a clear patch of ground and side-slipped towards it, with stick fully back and full top rudder. There was no time to lower the undercarriage, and with the desert surface pitted and rock-strewn an attempted wheels-down landing would probably have proved fatal anyway.

He levelled out and the Hurricane floated for an eternity, the ground blurring beneath its wings. Dead ahead, something that looked like the remains of a stone wall loomed out of the arid landscape.

Feather almost closed his eyes in despair. Nothing mattered now but sheer naked instinct. He pulled the stick back, knowing that he was going to hit the wall but pulling it back anyway in a last, desperate attempt to cushion the inevitable impact. Time stood still, and for a weird moment it seemed as though he were outside the cockpit, looking down on himself. Strange thoughts passed through his mind. In a detached sort of way, he wondered how he was going to die; whether his head would smash into the gunsight and burst open like a rotten apple, or whether his body would be crushed by

the engine as it came tearing back through the cockpit.

The Hurricane struck the wall tail-down with a bone-
jarring crunch, sending masonry and dust flying in all
directions. Feather put his arms up in front of his face
as the brutal deceleration slammed him forward in his
straps. The fighter's tail broke off a couple of feet aft of
the cockpit and the rest of the aircraft slewed across the
ground in its own miniature sandstorm, skidding violently
as a wingtip struck a boulder and shattered, shedding
fragments of aluminium.

There was a heavy silence, broken only by a metallic
crackling sound from the dead engine. Feather, dazed and
stunned, slowly became aware of his surroundings. Still
in slow motion, or so it seemed, he reached up to open
the cockpit hood and found to his amazement that it was
already open. He couldn't remember having opened it.

He pulled off his helmet, unfastened his straps and tried
to stand up, only to flop back down again. He placed both
hands on the cockpit rail and tried again, heaving himself
upright, standing on his parachute pack. His legs were
trembling and unsteady.

He tumbled out of the cockpit onto the crumpled
remains of the wing, sliding off it into the dust, searching
frantically for some shelter. He saw a shell crater thirty
yards away and stumbled towards it, still dazed and
staggering. He tripped over some stones and fell headlong
into the crater just as German shells began exploding
around the wreck of the Hurricane. Dimly, and with
considerable relief, his befogged brain registered the fact
that if the Germans were firing at his aircraft, he must

have come down inside the perimeter. He curled up into a ball, making himself as small as possible, burying his head in his arms, and waited for the barrage to cease.

Gradually, the volume of shellfire decreased until finally it stopped altogether. Cautiously, spitting out dust, Feather raised his head above the lip of the crater. His Hurricane, even more battered now, was burning fiercely.

Feather looked around. Although he knew that he was inside the perimeter, he had no idea which way to go. A wrong turn, and he might easily stumble into an enemy position. The front line could not be far away, he reasoned, or the enemy artillery spotters would not have been able to direct gunfire onto his aircraft so quickly.

His dilemma was solved for him by the sudden appearance of a helmeted head from behind a rock, fifty yards away. A sunburned arm waved at him.

"C'mon, mate," an unmistakeably Australian voice shouted. "Over here, and get a move on!"

Feather clawed his way out of the crater and started to run, his legs still feeling like rubber. He had not gone more than ten yards when there was the high-pitched chatter of a German machine-gun. Fountains of dust and stones sprayed into the air around him and something that felt like a white-hot poker lanced through his left thigh. He fell to the ground and cried out, clutching himself and rolling from side to side in pain.

He was conscious of being lifted, and of being hoisted on to someone's back in a 'fireman's lift'. His rescuer broke into a jolting run, and as he ran a trail of red blotches appeared on the ground behind him. With surprise and shock, Feather realised that it must be his own blood. Then he passed out.

He came to in a dugout. A face swam into focus before him, and he was conscious that someone was doing something to his leg.

A hand that presumably belonged to the same body as the face held a mess tin to his lips, and brackish water that tasted wonderful trickled between his lips.

"Y'all right, mate?" the face said. Feather nodded weakly.

"Well, yer thigh's busted. Yer won't be goin' flyin' fer a while. We'll have you out of here shortly."

Feather managed to speak. "Thanks. And thanks for bringing me in."

"Oh, that's all right, mate. No trouble. You were as light as a feather. Hey, what's the joke?"

Eight

Monday, 21 July 1941: the Front Line

"The desert is like a sea, don't you agree, Schmidt?" The sudden question posed by *General* Erwin Rommel took his personal aide, *Hauptmann* Heinz Werner Schmidt, by surprise. He had been half-dozing in the front seat of the open staff car, where he sat next to the driver; they had set out early from Rommel's headquarters in Bardia to make a tour of the front-line positions at Sollum, and Schmidt was short of an hour or so of his customary sleep. He half-turned and looked questioningly at his commander.

"Herr General?"

"Like the sea," Rommel repeated. "The battle in the desert resembles a battle at sea. Whoever has the weapons with the longest range, and whoever has the greater mobility, will win. Now we have the long-range weapons. Soon we will have the mobility."

Schmidt knew that Rommel was referring to the 88mm flak guns which were arriving in North Africa in growing numbers. Used as anti-tank weapons, they were devastating. In the early stages of the campaign, the shells of the smaller-calibre 37mm guns had simply bounced off the armour of the British Matilda tanks; now it would be a different story.

Rommel had bitter memories of the heavily-armoured Matilda. In May 1940, his 7th Armoured Division, in its headlong dash across France to the Channel coast, had been subjected to a strong British counter-attack near Arras, spearheaded by seventy-six Matilda tanks. The sudden onslaught by the British armour threw Rommel's infantry – the 7th Armoured Division's Rifle Regiments and the supporting troops of the SS *Totenkopf* Division – into total confusion, as Rommel later told in his own words.

"The enemy tank fire had created chaos among our troops, and they were jamming up the roads and yards with their vehicles instead of going into action with every available weapon to fight off the enemy. We tried to create order. The crew of a howitzer battery, some distance away, now left their guns, swept along by the retreating infantry. With *Leutnant* Most's help, I brought every available gun into action against the tanks. Every gun, both anti-tank and anti-aircraft, was ordered to open rapid fire immediately and I personally gave each gun its target. When the enemy tanks came perilously close, only rapid fire from every gun could save the situation."

The German anti-tank gunners were horrified to see their shells bouncing off the Matildas' armour, and when the infantry saw that their anti-tank guns were useless, those that were not killed or captured began to run, throwing away their weapons in their panic. After the battle, the British Tank Brigade commander, Brigadier Douglas Pratt, told how the Matildas:

". . . played hell with a lot of Boche motor transport and their kindred stuff. Tracer ammunition put a lot up in flames. His anti-tank gunners, after firing a bit, bolted and left their guns, even when fired on at ranges of six to eight hundred yards from Matildas. Some surrendered and others feigned dead on the ground. None of his anti-tank stuff penetrated our Is and IIs, and not even did his field artillery which fired high explosive. Some tracks were broken, and a few tanks were put on fire by his tracer bullets, chiefly in the engine compartment of the Matilda Is. One Matilda had fourteen direct hits from his 37mm guns, and it had no harmful effect, just gouged out a bit of armour.

"The main opposition came from his field guns, some of which fired over open sights. Also the air dive-bombing on the infantry – this, of course, did not worry the tanks much. One or two bombs bursting alongside a Matilda turned it over and killed the commander; another lifted a light tank about fifteen feet in the air. Had we only been able to stage a methodical battle with a series of reasonably short objectives, with some artillery support and even a little air support and no frantic rush, we should have done far better and saved many lives of fellows we cannot affort to lose . . ."

In fact the British thrust came to a halt when it came up against the 88mm anti-aircraft guns, hastily turned into anti-tank weapons on Rommel's orders and fired over open sights. Not even the Matildas' weight of armour could withstand their high-velocity shells, one of which was capable of blowing a Matilda's turret clean off.

Faced with a mere handful of the redoubtable 88mm

guns, the British attack ground to a halt just as it was about to complete a semi-circle around Arras. Nevertheless, the cost to the 7th *Panzer* Division had been heavy: 89 men killed, 116 wounded, 173 missing and 400 taken prisoner. On this one day alone, Rommel's division had suffered four times the losses it had sustained in the initial breakthrough across the Meuse. The British attack had achieved such complete surprise that at one stage Rommel thought he was being confronted by no fewer than five divisions.

It was all in vain. The armoured assault was to have been followed up by an infantry attack, but it never happened. Although the British attack had given the Germans a bloody nose and worried them sufficiently to make them hesitate in their forward drive, the British Expeditionary Force was not strong enough to exploit its advantage by breaking through the Germans completely and presenting a serious threat to their lines of communication. That night the *Luftwaffe* intervened, with dive-bombers making a series of heavy attacks on the villages held by the British infantry. The troops could only weather the storm as best they could, loosing off bursts of small arms fire and cursing the lack of RAF support. In the wake of the air assault, strong forces of German infantry attacked the villages held by the British troops, and before dark it became clear that these could no longer be held. Major General Harold Franklyn, the architect of the counter-attack, therefore decided that he had no option but to order a withdrawal. Later, he recorded that:

"... At the end of the day, my uppermost feeling

was one of bitter disappointment. I had been so hopeful earlier and now so little seemed to have been achieved. The capture of four hundred prisoners appeared a small reward for so much effort. I had, at the time, no conception of the extent to which the counter-attack around Arras had put the cat among the German pigeons . . ."

But Rommel had, and the battle of Arras had a profound effect on his tactical thinking. Never again would he leave his flanks unsecured, and never again would he allow his tanks to race on ahead and leave their supporting infantry virtually unprotected.

It soon became clear to *Hauptmann* Schmidt why Rommel had likened the desert war to a sea battle. He repeated the comparison a while later, addressing a conference of company commanders at Halfaya.

"Your troops at Halfaya Pass are immobile," he told them, while Schmidt – as was his duty – wrote furiously, making notes of the commander's words. "Only when they are in strong and well-prepared positions are they of value against motorised troops. But here again, the 'longest arm' has the advantage – and you now have it, in the shape of the 88-millimetre gun. It is essential for you, as static troops, to have the best-prepared cover, the best camouflage possible, and the best field of fire for your eighty-eights."

He slammed his clenched fist into the palm of his other hand, as though to ephasise his words.

"It is my intention to occupy a long defensive line stretching from the sea to Sidi Omar," he said, naming a location well to the south of Sollum. "Because of the distance involved the outpost positions, up to company strength, will have to be fairly far apart, but the whole line must be planned with a view to adequate defence in depth. Every strongpoint must be a complete defensive system in itself; every weapon must be sited so that it can be fired in any direction. In my opinion, the ideal arrangement would be on these lines."

Crouching down, Rommel rapidly drew a sketch map in the sand.

"One 88mm gun should be sunk into the ground as deeply as the field of fire permits. From here, trenches should radiate in three directions to three points – one a machine-gun position, the second a heavy mortar position, and the third either a light 20mm anti-aircraft gun or a 50mm anti-tank gun. Sufficient water, ammunition and supplies for three weeks must always be available, and every men is to be ready for action at all times, even when asleep. How are you off for ammunition and supplies?"

The question was addressed to one of the company commanders.

"Plenty of ammunition, *Herr General*, but food for only three days."

"Three days?" Rommel said, straightening up. "So. Never mind, we will attend to that. Make a note, Schmidt. Immediate action."

Privately, Rommel was becoming increasingly worried about the supply position, as Schmidt was aware. Soon he would be in command of a full *Panzergruppe* of five divisions, three German and two Italian, all of which would have to be supplied from bases on the other side of the Mediterranean; and until Tobruk was captured the supplies would have to be brought in through the ports of Tripolitania, which meant that the supply routes themselves remained vulnerable to the Malta-based submarines and aircraft. The losses inflicted on the supply convoys were already being referred to as 'catastrophic' by the Italians, as mostly it was their ships that were suffering, and they were calling for the *Luftwaffe* to return to Sicily urgently, so that a massive air offensive against Malta could be resumed.

"As for battle tactics," Rommel went on, "in the case of an enemy attack our arcs of gunfire must completely cover the gaps between the strong points. Should the enemy break through the gaps in conditions of bad visibility, for example, every weapon must be capable of engaging targets towards the rear. Every individual position must continue to hold, regardless of the general situation, until the *Panzer* and motorised infantry units in the rear are able to join the battle and destroy the enemy. Even if you should have no news of them for several weeks, do not worry; our armoured and motorised formations will not leave you in the lurch. Thank you, gentlemen. That will be all."

The company commanders snapped to attention, saluted and went off to their various tasks. Rommel and Schmidt returned to their staff car and resumed their tour of the front-line positions. Schmidt noted that his commander was in high good humour today, laughing even when a few British artillery shells burst nearby as they drove down 'Hellfire Pass' towards the coastal plain. His good mood improved even more when he noticed that at some defended points on the coastal plain, captured British tanks had been sunk deeply in the ground with only their turrets showing.

When they reached the coast Schmidt suggested a dip in the Mediterranean. Some troops in the vicinity stared in disbelief as their commander-in-chief, newly promoted to full general at the age of forty-nine, stripped off his dusty uniform and plunged into the sparkling sea, closely followed by his staff officer, both of them laughing like teenagers.

The troops had never seen a general behave like that before.

Afterwards, as they sat on the beach and let the hot sun dry them before resuming their journey, Rommel reflected on the events of the past weeks. When he had first assumed command of the *Afrika Korps*, he had wondered why Hitler and the German High Command had refused to pour *Panzer* divisions, artillery and supplies into North Africa – all the material that would have enabled him to gain a quick and decisive victory over the British.

Then had come the invasion of Russia, and suddenly Rommel had realised the future that Hitler was planning – a future which, after Russia was defeated, would see a victorious *Wehrmacht* plunging on into the Middle East, perhaps even following in the footsteps of Alexander the Great on the road to India. Now that would really be something!

Rommel was full of enthusiasm for the Russian venture, and confident of rapid victory. Some of his subordinate commanders did not share his confidence. One of them was *Oberst* Count Gerhard von Schwerin, who upon hearing of the German invasion quietly told his staff: "That's that. Now we have lost the war."

At least, the invasion of Russia had put Rommel's

task in Libya firmly into perspective. He would capture Tobruk first, then investigate ways of invading Egypt from the west. The armies in Russia, after conquering the Caucasus, would descend on Egypt from the north-east. Rommel had already drafted a plan for such a venture. All he had to do was to hold on tight in Africa until the Russian campaign was over; then the great pincer movement on Egypt could begin.

But Tobruk, so far, had doggedly refused to be captured, and remained a festering thorn in Rommel's flesh. He was already planning another major attack on the fortress, but he would not be in a position to mount it until November. Meanwhile, he would continue to strengthen the Sollum front, both as an insurance against a British offensive and to provide a sound jumping-off point for his own planned drive into Egypt after Tobruk was in his hands.

For the attack on Tobruk itself, Rommel envisaged a change of tactics. The next attack would be launched against the south-eastern sector of the perimeter and the weight of it would be borne by his two *Panzer* divisions, the 15th and 21st, both of which had already been withdrawn from the front for a much-needed rest and for specialist training. This move, however, had created its own set of problems. The 115th Rifle Regiment, part of 15th *Panzer*, which had been in the trenches at Tobruk ever since Rommel's first dash across the desert in April, had been pulled back to the coast east of Tobruk, and the sudden change of diet had proved disastrous; 70 per cent of the men were down with dysentery or jaundice, and it would be weeks before they were fit again.

Rommel had issued one order that had not endeared him to the troops besieging Tobruk. In an attempt to cause the garrison to waste much of its precious ammunition, he had ordered the erection of hundreds of dummy observation posts, made of wood and sacking, in areas that were unoccupied by the Germans. When a commander had plucked up the courage to ask where the wood was to be found in the desert, Rommel had told him to use his initiative, and had given fourteen days for the task to be completed.

Rommel's penchant for issuing unreasonable orders was legendary, and much resented. He was also inconsistent; he had a habit of threatening any officer with a court martial who, in his opinion, had failed to complete his mission in action, and then revoking the threat almost immediately. On one occasion, he recommended a battalion commander for the Knight's Cross, then charged him with cowardice and relieved him of his command, all within a few days.

Rommel was aware of all this, and of the fact that the new Italian commander in North Africa, General Ettore Bastico – a personal friend of Mussolini – did not like him. Rommel had got on quite well with Bastico's predecessor, General Italo Gariboldi, an affable, avuncular old buffer who could be easily manipulated, but Bastico was a different kettle of fish. Difficult, autocratic and with a quick temper, he had summoned Rommel to his headquarters a few days ago and informed the German that he, Bastico, was the supreme commander in North Africa, and that consequently he would not have his authority usurped by a relative newcomer. Rommel, smarting as a result of the encounter, had promptly nicknamed the Italian *Bombastico*.

But Rommel would have the last laugh. He was determined that the Italians would play little or no part in the assault on Tobruk; German troops would be pulled out of the defensive lines for the battle, their places being taken by Italian soldiers supported by a few German companies at vulnerable points.

"*Alarm! Fliegeralarm!*"

The sudden warning shout dragged Rommel out of his reverie and jerked Schmidt, who had been dozing, fully awake. Almost before they had time to move, a dark shadow flickered across the beach, accompanied by the roar of an engine. The looked up just in time to see a Hurricane, flying very low, heading out to sea. Rommel wondered why it had not opened fire.

The Hurricane flew on for some distance before turning towards the coast again to approach Tobruk from the seaward side. A few minutes later it touched down on the airstrip – which, by some miracle, had not yet been subjected to air attack – and a sweat-drenched Eamonn O'Day climbed from the cockpit. He made for the stone hut, where he was greeted by Flight Lieutenant Johnson. O'Day was clutching a notepad on which he had scribbled the observations he had made during his tactical reconnaissance sortie.

"Good trip?" Johnson asked.

"Not bad. Things are pretty quiet. A spot of light flak at Maddalena, but nothing to worry about."

O'Day's flight had taken him from Tobruk south-east across the Dahar Er-Rhegem table-land and a series of desert depressions as far as the enemy-occupied airstrip at Maddalena, where he had sighted a few *Stukas*, then northwards along the front line that was being established along the Egyptian frontier up to Sollum. Carefully, he and Johnson plotted the information he had brought back on to a map. As they were finishing their task, drawing little circles around enemy strongpoints near Sollum, O'Day suddenly chuckled.

"What's tickling you?" Johnson wanted to know.

"Oh, nothing at all, really. As I was crossing the coast I spotted a couple of blokes lying on the beach, bollock naked. They were obviously Huns or Eyeties, because the Arabs don't strip off in public. I could easily have given 'em a squirt, but it just didn't seem fair, somehow. Wonder who they were?"

Nine

Tobruk: 16 August 1941. Dusk.

By the middle of August, the Tobruk perimeter – and in particular the embattled western sector – was showing all the signs of four months of siege. The no man's land between the forward posts was thickly carpeted with mines and booby traps, and strewn with the unburied bodies of the dead of both sides, bodies impossible to reach, bleached and desiccated in the sun. Some were no more than skeletons, for the rats had feasted well . . .

The defences, if such they could be called, were still in the same primitive condition: narrow and shallow trenches in which there was no room for the occupants to sit or kneel. The defenders had taken up their positions in the previous night and had been here all day, for movement during the hours of daylight was impossible. Once the sun had risen, the defenders could not move out, nor could reserves and supplies get up to them.

But now it was dusk, and time for the unofficial two-hour truce. During this period, neither side opened fire on the other and the troops on both sides could emerge safely from their cramped positions. Food, water and ammunition could be brought up to the forward defensive positions.

There were grimmer matters to be attended to. From the Australian positions a truck moved slowly forward. A soldier stood on the bonnet, waving a large Red Cross flag. No shots were fired. Four hundred yards on, some 250 yards from the German forward positions, the truck halted on the edge of a minefield and three men dismounted. Two were stretcher-bearers; the other a padre.

A German soldier rose from a foxhole, also waving a Red Cross flag, and shouted *"Achtung, Minen!"* The warning was unnecessary; the bodies of thirteen Australian soldiers sprawled in the sand provided warning enough.

Two Germans emerged with a mine detector and guided an officer and a doctor out to the Australian stretcher party. The man in charge of the latter, a sergeant, told the doctor that they had come to pick up the Australian dead and wounded. The doctor nodded and replied in English.

"Very well, but only two men at a time. You must not come any closer than this. We will send out your wounded."

They brought out four Australian wounded and allowed the truck to come forward a little so that they could be loaded on board. Then they brought out the bodies of fifteen dead, and helped to recover the thirteen corpses from the minefield. The dead were stacked in the back of the truck like sardines; the padre, head bowed, prayed over them.

When the last of the Australian dead had been loaded,

the German lieutenant told the stretcher-bearers that they were to stay where they were until the German soldiers were back in their posts. As his men disappeared into their foxholes, the lieutenant turned and lowered his flag; the Australian sergeant did the same and the two men exchanged salutes.

A few minutes later, a burst of tracer bullets rose into the air from the German positions. It was the signal that, for tonight, the truce was over.

For those who fought at Tobruk, defenders and besiegers alike, life was an eternal, savage battle against insects. At night, following the legions of flies that made daylight hours a torment, came the sand fleas: the vicious, hardy desert vermin that crawled in an itching, stabbing procession over a man's body after nightfall until he thought he would go crazy from lack of sleep. One soldier recorded in his diary:

"All day we lay in a dugout just big enough for three diggers and me. Four feet above us was a roof of corrugated iron resting on sleepers and over that sandbags, earth and bits of camel-bush, which made the dugout just one more piece of desert to German snipers scanning the level plain from five hundred yards away. The late afternoon sun beat down on the sandbags. We were clammy with sweat. The wind died away and dust stopped drifting in through the small air vent and the narrow low doorway that led to the crawl trench outside. The air was heavy with dust, cigarette smoke and the general fug we'd been breathing in and out for the past thirteen hours. We waited for darkness when we could fill our lungs with fresh, cool air, and the troops could crack at the Hun who had been lying all day in his dugout, too.

"I woke about seven in the evening and started to scratch. I seemed to be itching all over – the itchiness of being dirty. You get that way after the flies and fleas have been at you all day. You don't know whether you've been bitten or not, and you just scratch as a matter of routine. In the far corner Mick was doing a bit of hunting. He had his shirt off. Seriously, deliberately he ran his thumb nail under the seam and a slow smile of success spread across his face. 'Got you, you little bastards! That makes four less, anyway!'"

The pilots and ground crews of Armstrong's squadron were gradually learning to live with the pests. They were far luckier than the troops; at least they did not have to spend their days in sweltering dugouts on the perimeter. Those on readiness lived in tents on the airstrip for a day at a time, close to their sandbagged, camouflaged Hurricanes, the latter maintained by the small nucleus of ground personnel; some of the latter had been in Tobruk since the port was first taken from the Italians, and seemed to have come to terms with the living conditions there. One armourer, a stocky corporal from Liverpool, kept a small menagerie of lizards and tame mice.

"The lizard's one of our best friends, sir," he explained one day to Don Petrie. "Watch." He pointed to a large desert sore on his leg, on the fringes of which bloated flies were clustered like pigs around a feeding trough, and brought one of his pet lizards close to it, stroking the creature's palpitating flank with the tip of his index finger. An instant later the lizard's long tongue flicked out, and the flies appeared as if by magic. "See what I mean?" he said cheerfully. The New Zealander felt slightly sick, but took the point.

The pilots soon discovered that the mice, too, were highly functional. The trick was to put a couple of the creatures in one's sleeping bag for half an hour after turning in, if one could tolerate their scrabblings, and then set them free; usually the fleas would have migrated to the mice from their human hosts, permitting at least an hour or two of sleep. The mice seemed to suffer no ill effects; on the contrary, they thrived on human care and attention, and some became so tame that they even answered to their names. Fantastic stakes were laid on mouse races, in which the mice proved exceptionally unco-operative.

The RAF personnel also learned to be constantly on guard against scorpions, deadly pests which were killed on sight. They were so hated that sometimes, when one was caught, it would be dropped into the middle of a bit of paper, which was then set alight around the edges; the troops would look on gleefully as the scorpion, with no escape from the flames, stabbed itself to death.

It was not an exercise which the pilots, faced with the ever-present prospect of being burnt alive, particularly relished.

Desert centipedes, which grew to an amazing size, were less obvious pests; although relatively harmless, they had to be removed from exposed skin with great care. One of the airmen brushed a centipede off his arm in the opposite direction to that in which the insect was travelling, and had a long strip of skin ripped away by the creature's hooked claws. The wound turned septic, and the man needed hospital treatment.

On General Morshead's orders, Armstrong had restricted his squadron's activities mainly to tactical reconnaissance sorties during the past couple of weeks. These were usually flown at dawn or last light, to reduce the risk of running into enemy fighters, and pilots were briefed to keep within a fifty-mile radius of the Tobruk perimeter and to avoid the airfield at Gambut, where the enemy had built up a considerable concentration of aircraft. Occasionally, longer reconnaissance flights – such as the one just completed by O'Day – were also requested, and sometimes the pilots were ordered to fly out to sea, ranging eastwards as far as the Gulf of Sollum in search of overdue vessels on the 'Spud Run', as the Navy's supply operation was nicknamed.

It was the ships of the Royal Navy's Mediterranean Inshore Squadron that bore the brunt of supplying the besieged Tobruk garrison, and the heaviest burden of all was carried by the Anglo-Australian destroyers of the 10th Destroyer Flotilla, bringing in supplies from Alexandria or Mersa Matruh. In the beginning there had been seven destroyers, five of them Australian – HMAS *Stuart, Vampire, Vendetta, Voyager* and *Waterhen* – and two British, HMS *Defender* and *Decoy*. The Australian boats were elderly vessels and the reconnaissance pilots came to know them all, feeling an upsurge of affection and admiration whenever they caught sight of one of them, ploughing her way westwards from Alexandria. Day after day they battled their way through, fighting off the enemy bombers that sometimes attacked them as they made their lone runs under cover of darkness. Hardly a destroyer reached the garrison without being attacked, and inevitably there were losses. On twenty-nine June *Waterhen* was sunk off Bardia, together with an accompanying sloop, *Auckland*, and on twelve July *Defender* was lost off Sidi Barani. The others continued to bear charmed lives, breaking the Axis blockade to bring in supplies and fresh troops, evacuating the battle-weary and the wounded.

Other ships were not so lucky. As the months went by, the Inshore Squadron acquired an extraordinary collection of craft, including battered, rusting Greek steamers, captured Italian schooners and angular, strange-looking vessels which the Navy called 'A' Lighters. They were the forerunners of the tank landing craft that would later form the spearhead of the Allied invasion of occupied Europe. They carried not only tanks to Tobruk, but also dangerous cargoes of petrol, mines and ammunition. They were painfully slow and ill-armed, and the passage through 'Bomb Alley' – that most heavily attacked stretch of coast between Sollum and Bardia – was a nightmare for their crews.

Some of the tramp steamers on the 'Spud Run' took a fearful hammering. Early one morning, Dickie Baird, who was on standby, took off to try to locate a Greek ship which, having successfully made the run through Bomb Alley, was reportedly being attacked by enemy aircraft several miles to the west of Tobruk, having apparently overshot the harbour during the night. He had no difficulty in finding the vessel, for its position was marked by a tall column of smoke, stark and black in the dawn sky. The aircraft had gone, leaving the ship listing and in flames, and yet the crew were still making desperate attempts to save her. It was a hopeless battle. Baird circled the stricken freighter, watching helplessly as her list increased. Suddenly, more smoke, shot with vivid flame, boiled up as an explosion ripped her foredeck apart. After that, it was all over in seconds. The ship turned over, exposing her rusted, barnacle-encrusted bottom, and slid tiredly under the surface, leaving a spreading pool of burning fuel oil and a handful of struggling survivors. Baird passed a fix over the radio and continued to circle the spot until his fuel ran dangerously low, compelling him to return to base. He later learned that a destroyer had steamed to the spot with all speed, but that no survivors had been picked up.

Now, on this night in mid-August, something big was happening in Tobruk. Shortly after dark the fast minelayer HMS *Abdiel* nosed her way into the cluttered harbour. She carried several hundred men of the Polish Carpathian Brigade, the advance guard of 6,000 Poles and troops of the British 70th Division, a formation that included battalions of regiments with proud battle honours – regiments like the Durham Light Infantry and the Black Watch.

In the darkness, as the fresh troops moved up to take their positions, the Australians began to move out. They moved down the wadis in single file, marching slowly, out of step, in the silence of exhaustion, only the dull clink of their weapons sounding in the night air. Even in daylight it would have been hard to tell one man's face from the face of the man in front of or behind him. All their faces were burnt almost black, fringed by several days' growth of stubble. Their cheeks were hollow, their eyes red-rimmed, with the whites gleaming. Their shirts and shorts were stiff, like canvas, with mingled dust and sweat, their boots scrubbed almost pure white by the scouring sand. Their packs, haversacks and ammunition pouches were white too, bleached by the sun, the stocks of their rifles and tommy-guns shining and polished through constant use.

These were the men used to the almost daily taunts of William Joyce, 'Lord Haw-Haw', the Irish traitor whose nasal drawl was carried across Europe and the Mediterranean by the transmitters of Berlin Radio.

"Good morning, rats. How are you this morning? Not very well, I hope. And how is your air force? Oh, I forgot, you haven't got one, have you? Never mind, we have plenty of planes, so we'll send a few over for you. It can't be very nice over there, cowering like rats in your holes. That's what you are, you know. Rats. And do you know what we do with rats? We exterminate them."

But these were the men of the 9th Australian Infantry Division, who had resisted all the enemy's attempts to exterminate them. And Lord Haw-Haw had unwittingly bestowed upon them a title that would proudly echo down the years.

They were the desert rats. The Rats of Tobruk.

Armstrong assembled his pilots an hour before dawn. By some miracle they were all still there, apart from Feather, who had been evacuated.

"As you will have gathered," he said, "the Aussies are

being relieved at last. They've been here five months, and they're just about at the end of their tether. I like to think our presence here has given them a bit of a boost. The point is that as soon as the Huns find out what's going on they'll go all out to knock seven bells out of the ships bringing the troops in and out. Its up to us to stop them. General Morshead has asked us to lay on a maximum effort. As the operation is likely to last for up to ten days, it doesn't look as though we shall be getting much in the way of sleep."

Somebody groaned, and Armstrong knew exactly how he felt. He paused to let the information sink in, then went on:

"One thing is pretty certain. We can expect the airstrip to come under attack. I'm surprised it hasn't happened already; perhaps they think we aren't much of a threat, since we've been carrying out Tac-R sorties rather than intercepting their raids. But all that is bound to change, and so the general has had a secondary strip prepared for us. It's in a wadi on the south side of the Derna road, about a mile out of town. It's being stocked up with fuel and ammo, and we should be able to sustain operations for about a week if the strip here is knocked out. Remember – if you are returning from a sortie and find this strip under attack, make for the secondary. Any questions so far?"

"Any idea how much warning time we'll have, sir?" It was van Berg who posed the question.

"Not much, I'm afraid," Armstrong replied. "Indications are that the main weight of the attack will come from Gambut, which as you know is only thirty-five miles away. We can't expect much help, either. Our nearest advanced landing grounds are a hundred and twenty miles away, and although the squadrons there might be able to send out the odd flight of Hurricanes with long-range tanks, that will be it."

After the short briefing, the pilots had a meal of tinned bacon and fried bread; hardly the ideal food in conditions where constant thirst was the main factor, but all there was. As dawn broke they went out to their aircraft. There was nothing to do now but wait.

On the airfield at Gambut *Capitano* Umberto Ricci and the pilots of the 15th Squadron waited too. He had been roused from a deep sleep by an orderly half an hour earlier, and was not in the best of humour.

"Everyone is to report immediately to the group commander's tent," the orderly had told him. There's a big circus on today."

Despite the orderly's warning, Ricci hoped that the day's operations would not be too strenuous. One of his flight commanders was due to celebrate his birthday that evening and a party had been planned, with cake, wine and brandy. Despite the fact that there would be no female company, which he regretted, Ricci was looking forward to the occasion.

The group commander, *Tenete Colonello* Pini, was waiting for them in his tent, seated behind a trestle table. He had seen some action in the Spanish Civil War, and none since then; without exception, all the pilots assembled before him were more experienced than he was. In order to have been appointed to command the group, he must have friends in high places. Ricci, who did not like him, was certain of that. Pini was a heavy-featured man, tending to run to fat, even though he was only in his early thirties. He was balding, and when he addressed someone he had the most annoying habit of staring over their head.

He wasted no time on preliminaries. As soon as all the pilots were gathered around him in a semi-circle, he said:

"Gentlemen, today the whole of our available air power will launch a major attack on Tobruk, where the garrison, according to our intelligence sources, is in the process of being relieved. Our orders, received late last night directly from the C-in-C, *Generale* Bastico, are quite specific. During the course of the day, we are to destroy every fighter aircraft available to the enemy inside the Tobruk perimeter."

Ricci permitted himself a wry inward smile at Pini's use of the word 'we'. He knew that the group commander would not be flying on operations. He never did.

"This task is to be accomplished as quickly as possible," Pini continued. "Afterwards, in addition to our normal bomber escort role, which we will undertake in case the enemy sends up more fighters from across the border, we will carry out fighter sweeps over Tobruk in between the bomber raids, attacking targets of opportunity – in particular, anti-aircraft emplacements."

He glanced at his watch. "Beginning at oh-seven-hundred today," he said, "one hundred bombers will operate over Tobruk at ten-minute intervals. Each relay will consist of approximately ten aircraft escorted by twice as many fighters. All the fighters," he proclaimed proudly, his chest puffing out like a pouter pigeon's, "will be provided by the *Regia Aeronautica*. We will be called upon to fly four, maybe five sorties over Tobruk in the course of the day. I have no doubt at all that we are equal to the task."

That 'we' again, Ricci thought, only half listening as Pini rumbled on. Afterwards, he drew the pilots of his 15th Squadron to one side.

"Listen," he said, "you all know what I think about ground strafing through heavy flak. We lost too many pilots over Malta doing just that. So, what I'm saying to you is – no heroics, and that's an order. Go in low and fast, shoot up whatever is in front of you and get out. Some of us, the older hands that is, are sometimes tempted to push our luck. We get the feeling we're immune. Well, we are not. Do not, under any circumstances, attempt a second run over the target, even though you don't hit anything on your first pass. I want us all back for the party tonight. Especially you, Tagliotti." He glared at his flight commander, the birthday boy, who grinned sheepishly.

On the other side of the airfield a squadron of German *Stukas* was already running up its engines. They would be first off, followed by the three squadrons of the Italian fighter group. The 15th Squadron would be the last to go.

By the time it was the turn of Ricci's squadron to take off the first Stukas and Macchis were already returning. Ricci noticed, grimly, that three of the German aircraft were missing and that some of the others had sustained battle damage. Whatever was happening over Tobruk, it was clearly no picnic. All the Macchis had returned in one piece, though, which was encouraging.

Ricci's pilots climbed into the cockpits of their Macchis. A mechanic, standing on the wing beside the cockpit, helped Ricci to fasten his straps and attach his oxygen and radio-telephone leads. The man shouted something, and Ricci lifted the flap of his helmet in order to hear better.

"Get a couple for me, sir!"

The pilot grinned in acknowledgement and operated the switches in the cockpit as the mechanic cranked the handle on the starting-trolley. The 870hp Fiat A74 radial engine kicked over a few times and then burst into full-throated life. Ricci checked his instruments carefully to make sure everything was in order, then waved away the chocks and released the brakes. The Macchi taxied forward, flanked by two others. As usual, the squadron was putting up nine aircraft, which would be flying in three sections of three.

Ricci pulled back on the throttle and the Macchi moved forward with the other two keeping pace, their wingtips no more than fifteen feet apart, gathering speed over the bumpy, sandy ground. (Ricci understood that the British and Germans pushed their throttles *forward* to increase power and pull them back to ease it off, a procedure which he thought very strange).

The rumbling of the fighter's wheels ceased abruptly and he was airborne. The three aircraft flashed over the airfield perimeter, their shadows fleeting ahead of them over objects which by now had become so familiar since the move from Derna a few weeks earlier: the burnt-out wreck of a Savoia bomber, the skeletal remains of a few trucks, worn out and cannibalised for spare parts.

The nine Macchis stayed as low as the terrain would allow, speeding along the road that led to Tobruk – a road built by Italian engineers. Over on the right, despite their low level, the sea was clearly visible, looking very inviting.

Ten minutes later the Italian fighters were roaring over the Tobruk perimeter, pursued by small arms fire, and there was no longer any time for sightseeing. Ahead, the harbour area and town were covered by a pall of smoke and dust. A few thousand feet higher up, drifting slowly on the wind, a host of flak bursts had mingled to form another, thinner smoke layer.

The ground beneath was criss-crossed with the scars of trenches and coiled lines of barbed wire. Ahead and above, a cluster of fresh anti-aircraft bursts indicated that a new bombing raid was going in. The bombers themselves were invisible, as were any fighters that might have been in action against them.

In front of the speeding Macchis now was an escarpment. German photo-reconnaissance aircraft had been active over Tobruk during the past few days, and Ricci had spent hours studying photographs of the defences. Photos of the airstrip on the escarpment had not revealed any aircraft, which must have been expertly camouflaged, but he knew they were there; their presence had been betrayed by recent tyre-marks on the strip itself, made by aircraft taking off and landing.

Suddenly, immediately ahead of him, he saw a fighter, a couple of hundred feet higher up. He identified it at once as a Hurricane, its undercarriage and flaps lowered. He was closing with it so fast that there was no time to alert the other pilots of his flight.

Someone must have alerted the Hurricane pilot to the approaching danger, though, for he made a desperate attempt to escape at the last moment, throwing his aircraft into a climbing turn and starting to retract his undercarriage. He was too late. Ricci pressed the triggers of his machine-guns, sending twin streams of 12.7mm bullets into the British aircraft just forward of its cockpit. Instantly, a great gush of flame burst from the Hurricane, enveloping the whole of the centre fuselage. The fighter, one undercarriage leg dangling, went ito a steep diving turn and ploughed into the ground, bursting apart in a bubble of fire.

Ricci streaked over the remains and suddenly found himself over the airstrip. A group of steel-helmeted figures swept into his field of vision, running for their lives, and he instinctively pressed the triggers again, seeing the ground around them erupt in fountains of dust. He did not see whether he had hit any of them. Apart from that, the airstrip was deserted.

The Macchis streaked on, still keeping low and heading for the coast. Safely out over the sea they curved to the right and flew parallel with the shoreline for a few miles before turning inland again and setting course for Gambut.

The Hurricane had been Ricci's first combat victory.

It had been ridiculously easy. If that was all there was to it, he had every chance of chalking up a respectable score in the weeks to come. He suddenly felt ten feet tall.

Ten

Friday, 22 August 1941. Tobruk

There were only six Hurricanes left now; six aircraft and seven pilots. Kostelas had died needlessly, trying to land his aircraft on the original airstrip instead of on the secondary, as Armstrong had ordered, and had been shot out of the sky by an Italian fighter patrol. A day or two later van Berg had broken both legs in a crash-landing and had been evacuated; and although there had been no further loss of life or injury, another precious Hurricane had been written off in a landing accident when Weston ran it into a bomb crater.

Now, on this Friday morning, Armstrong's weary pilots were airborne yet again, climbing hard to the east of Tobruk, searching for the incoming enemy bombers. Instead, they found the fighters. It was Kalinski who sighted them first.

"Look out, bandits astern, six and seven o'clock, high, closing fast. Jesus, they're one-oh-nines!"

The Pole was mistaken, although it was an easy error to make. The enemy fighters were Macchi C202s, new arrivals in North Africa, and at a distance their Alfa Romeo in-line engines made them resemble the German

Messerchmitt 109. As they drew closer, however, the differences between the two became apparent, the main one being that the Italian fighter's cockpit was set well back on the fuselage, above the trailing edge of the wing. The raised, enclosed cockpit gave the C202 a distinctive hump-backed appearance; in fact, it resembled the Hurricane more than it did the Me 109.

The Hurricane pilots waited a few moments, then Armstrong gave the order to break towards the enemy. There were about thirty of them, flying in sections of four. Inexplicably, they continued to fly straight ahead as the six Hurricanes swept past them and curved round behind their formation. It was only when the Hurricanes opened fire on the rearmost section that the Italians reacted.

The next few minutes were a whirling confusion of twisting aircraft. There was no time for co-ordinated tactics; with odds of six against thirty, it was every man for himself. At one point, Kalinski, intent on shooting down a Macchi, glanced in his rear-view mirror and saw half a dozen more, all jockeying for a position to take a shot at him. He pulled around in a tight turn, abandoning his intended victim, and met them head-on, missing the leading aircraft by a few inches as it swept over the top of him, buffeting the Hurricane with its slipstream. Another Macchi appeared off to one side, turning steeply towards him. Kalinski turned also, trying to cut inside the enemy, but it proved far more difficult than he had expected. These new Macchis were much more manoeuvrable than their radial-engined predecessors.

Every fibre of Kalinski's body ached with concentration as he strove to out-turn the enemy fighter. Despite the effort, every detail of the Macchi etched itself indelibly on his mind: the sandy camouflage mottled with dark green, the black *fasces* insignia of Mussolini's Italy, the white fuselage band. He was even close enough to discern the motif on the white band, a prancing black horse.

Kalinski had no idea how long the merry-go-round continued, but there came an instant when he knew, with sudden, blinding awareness, that he was not going to make it. The Macchi was gaining on him all the time; if he broke away the Italian would have him cold, and if he went on turning his adversary would soon be in a position to shoot his tail off.

Stainslaw, you bloody fool, he told himself, you've really done it this time. Suddenly, in desperation, without even considering the implications of the manoeuvre, he slammed the stick over to the left and at the same time kicked the left rudder pedal. The hard-pressed Hurricane, already teetering on the edge of a stall, flicked over on its back and literally fell out of the turn. Sand flew around the cockpit and for a few seconds Kalinski lost control completely as the Hurricane went into a violent spin.

The desert became a confused blur in front of his eyes and the horizon expanded to enfold him as the Hurricane continued to fall. He brought the fighter out of its headlong plunge at 3,000 feet and continued in a shallow, high-speed dive to ground level, turning on to a north-esterly heading as he did so and looking back over his shoulder.

The Macchi was still with him, half a mile or so astern and closing fast. Ahead of Kalinski, a broad, steep-walled wadi twisted away in roughly the direction he was going. He dropped into it, dangerously low, leap-frogging the sandy hummocks and piles of stone that raced towards him. His one chance was to run, in the hope that the Macchi pilot would eventually abandon the chase through shortage of fuel.

Fountains of sand and stones burst from the wadi wall beyond the Hurricane's port wingtip as the Macchi opened fire. Kalinski's heart was pounding. The Macchi was well within range, and he could imagine its pilot sitting tensed in the cockpit, waiting until he could be sure of his kill.

A mile in front of the speeding aircraft, the wadi split in two. In the fleeting seconds left to him, a desperate gamble took shape in Kalinski's mind. He held his breath as the fork in the dried-up river bed hurtled towards him, deliberately holding the Hurricane low and level, his slipstream kicking up a miniature sandstorm in his wake. Then, at the last moment, he stood the fighter on its tail.

So abrupt was the manoeuvre that for one brief, ter-rifying instant the Hurricane continued to skid forward, carried by its own momentum towards the sheer face of the cliff that stood at the centre of the wadi's fork. Then its propeller bit into the hot, dry air and the fighter rocketed upwards, gradually losing momentum as gravity fought against the power of its struggling Merlin engine.

Suddenly, the overworked Merlin blew up in Kalinski's

face with a terrific noise of tortured metal. A massive cloud of smoke enveloped the aircraft, which was still climbing. There was only one course of action, and Kalinski took it. By a stroke of luck his cockpit canopy was already open. Feverishly he unfastened his seat harness, took a deep breath and kicked the stick forward as hard as he could. He was only half aware of being catapulted violently from the cockpit.

The roaring, rending sounds of his doomed Hurricane were cut off abruptly and he was floating, spreadeagled on a cushion of air. He was falling on his back, the airflow plucking at his clothing. He moved an arm vaguely and his body rolled over gently until he was falling face down.

The desert was expanding to meet him. Jerked brutally back to reality, he gripped the D-ring of his parachute and pulled it hard. The drogue streamed from his parachute pack, pulling out the main canopy. It was not the first time he had baled out of a stricken aircraft – he had been forced to do so twice during the Polish campaign – but he still experienced the heart-stopping moments of uncertainty before the canopy deployed over his head with a sharp crack and the harness bit into his body, almost winding him.

Looking down, he could clearly see the spot where the wadi divided. From the foot of the cliff a dark column of smoke, its base shot with orange flame, rose like a tombstone. Around it lay the charred, fragmented wreckage of what had once been an aircraft. His desperate gamble had paid off: the Italian pilot, intent on his kill and half blinded by the sand whirled up by the speeding Hurricane, had failed to see the cliff in time to take avoiding action, and had paid for the error with his life.

Not that it's done me much good in the end, Kalinski told himself wryly, as he drifted down. A few moments later, as though to emphasise his predicament, he hit the ground with a thump that knocked all the breath out of him and temporarily stunned him. When he came to his senses, there was sand in his mouth and something soft and suffocating all around him. It felt as though his body were cocooned in a spider's web and for long moments he panicked irrationally, clawing blindly at the material and gasping for breath as he tried to struggle to his knees. His searching hands encountered parachute silk and he almost wept with relief as he realised that the waking nightmare was nothing more than the canopy. No breeze stirred the desert air and the silk had collapsed around him like a shroud.

He pushed the clinging folds aside cautiously and looked around him. He had no idea, at the moment, how far he was from Tobruk, but he seemed to be quite alone in the desert; his gaze encountered only sand and scrub and the remains of the Italian aircraft. Of his crashed Hurricane there was no sign. The Macchi was still burning fiercely, and he hoped fervently that the smoke would not attract unwanted visitors.

He felt his limbs carefully for broken bones, but apart from a few bruises he seemed to be uninjured. It was only when he stood up that he felt pain lance through his left ankle; it throbbed and nagged at him whenever he took a step, and he knew that he would not be able to walk far. The sensible thing, he told himself, would be to strap up his ankle and lie up until nightfall; perhaps the pain would have eased by then.

He gathered his parachute canopy into a heap, weighted it down with a rock, and limped over to inspect the wreck of the Macchi.

He did not linger long, his inspection cut short by the sight of the headless, limbless torso of the Italian pilot, lying some distance away from the shattered cockpit. For an uneasy moment, Kalinski felt that he was staring down at his own fate; then he shrugged off the macabre sensation, returned to his parachute and set about fashioning a makeshift tent between some rocks. Breathing hard with the effort, he crawled under the spread-out canopy, which would afford at least some protection from the high-intensity sunlight, and took stock of his situation.

He knew that he was somewhere to the south-east of Tobruk. He recalled that the Hurricanes had been about halfway between Tobruk and Gambut when they encountered the Italian fighters, and during the air battle he remembered seeing the Tobruk-Sollum road and the railway to the south of it. If his rough calculations were correct, that would put him exactly in the middle of nowhere, deep in enemy territory, about twenty miles from the coast and maybe thirty miles from the Tobruk perimeter.

It was not a rosy picture. There must be frequent enemy movements in the area to the north, between Tobruk and the front line; to move by day would risk almost certain detection, quite apart from the fact that he had no water and was in a semi-exhausted state. He decided to take a risk on the smoke from the crashed Macchi – which was now beginning to thin out – attracting an enemy patrol and to stay where he was until dark, when he would strike out north-eastwards, navigating by the stars.

He glanced at his watch; nightfall was over seven hours away, and he knew that he was in for a long and uncomfortable wait. He was already parched, and as the afternoon dragged on thirst became a torment. The utter silence played tricks on him, too; from time to time he fancied that he could hear voices, but it was only the rasp of his own breath as he sucked air into his lungs. By late afternoon his thirst was becoming unbearable. He placed a small pebble under his tongue. According to the RAF's desert survival booklet it was supposed to increase the flow of saliva. It didn't. It felt like a boulder and he spat it out with some difficulty, for his dehydrated tongue had begun to swell.

He must have dozed for a while, or at any rate lapsed into a kind of stupor. It seemed like only moments, but when he snapped fully awake again the air inside his parachute tent was not quite so suffocating and the shadows had lengthened. He crawled out into the open, under a sky aflame with one of the most glorious sunsets he had seen. Tired and tormented though he was, the sight took his breath away. The lower edge of an enormous red sun kissed the western horizon, and above it, like a crown, tiny flecks of cloud, high in the stratosphere, caught the rays and shone like drops of molten gold. From one end of the horizon to the other the sky glowed

with all the colours of the spectrum, a fantastic backdrop
to the dark, undulating line of the dunes.

Kalinski shivered. The temperature had already dropped noticeably, and he decided that he had better get
moving. Night came quickly in the desert, and the cold
would soon be intense. Using his penknife, he carved
a large square out of his parachute canopy and draped
it over his shoulders; it would provide some insulation
from the cold, and protection from the sun the next day.
He hestitated briefly, wondering whether to bury the rest
of his parachute, and then decided not to bother. Even if
an enemy patrol found it, he would be well on his way
and the chances of a lone man on foot being caught in
the darkness were slender. He left the parachute where
it was, together with his flying helmet, but retained the
tinted goggles. He also kept his .38 Smith and Wesson
Service revolver, which had been strapped to his thigh.
There were six rounds in the chamber.

He placed another small pebble under his tongue, and
this time, to his surprise and relief, he felt the inside of
his mouth moisten slightly. Perhaps, he thought, it was
something to do with the temperature drop. He set off
walking at a slow, steady pace, resisting the temptation
to hurry and tire himself out. Thankfully, the pain in his
ankle had been reduced to a nagging stiffness, which
grew less troublesome as he went on.

He trudged on, keeping the glow of the setting sun a
few degrees on his left. To his surprise he found that
he was walking on a flat, barren gravel plain, unbroken
except for a curious mound protruding from it, about a
mile from his starting point. There was a good deal of

light remaining, and as he drew closer he recognised the mound for what it was: the wreckage of his Hurricane.

The aircraft appeared to have struck in a flat attitude, a result, perhaps, of the fact that the engine was missing. It must have broken away completely as the Hurricane fell, and there was no sign of it. Conscious of a strong smell of petrol, Kalinski approached the wreck and climbed on to the stump of a wing. He reached down into the crumpled cockpit and eventually found what he was looking for: a small canvas pack, wedged into the pocket at the side of the cockpit where maps were normally stowed. His map was still there too, and he retrieved it along with the pack.

Already drooling in anticipation, he tore the pack open and reverently extracted a water bottle. It was still intact, apparently undamaged by the impact, its contents making a reassuring sloshing sound when he shook it.

He unscrewed the cap, raised the bottle to his lips and allowed a few drops of water to trickle down his parched throat. It was brackish, and tasted of chemicals. It was utterly beautiful.

His mouth and throat moistened, he drank more deeply, then forced himself to replace the cap. He felt suddenly wonderful, and ready to tackle anything. And all for the sake of a few drops of water, the one commodity on the planet that most people took for granted . . .

A small torch in the pack had not withstood the impact, but a pocket compass had. There was a bar of chocolate, too, and a few biscuits wrapped in greaseproof paper. Starvation would not be an immediate problem, but Kalinski realised how lucky he had been. If he had delayed his departure until it was fully dark, he might well have missed the crashed aircraft, to die a miserable death from thirst and hunger. That might still happen, his subconscious mind whispered to him, but your time is not yet. He pushed the precious water bottle back into the bag, slung the latter around his neck by its thin strap, and resumed his trek.

Ahead of him, the glow of the sunset gradually died away as he trudged on, and dark blue velvet crept over the sky from the east, brilliant with stars. The moon had not yet risen, but the stars themselves shed their light on the desert, enabling him to pick his way without much difficulty. The silence was overwhelming, the crunch of his desert boots sounding unnaturally loud on the gravel. He was glad of the boots; that was one valid piece of advice in the survival pamphlet. Always fly in the boots in which you intend walking home.

Despite the cold, he found himself sweating. His breath rasped in his throat, the walls of which were soon parched again, but he resisted the temptation to consume any more water. He planted one foot in front of the other stolidly, counting the steps and concentrating only on the few yards of ground in front of him.

He plodded on for an hour, two hours. All around him there was nothing but silence. Overhead, seeming to recede and then grow bright again in front of his eyes, the stars mocked him. Once or twice, he paused and looked around; the silver crescent of the moon was coming up over the horizon, its pale light casting weird shadows. He had the strange, unreal feeling of walking on water.

There was a subtle change in the crunching sound underfoot; it was becoming lighter and more brittle. Puzzled, he reached down and scooped up a handful of pebbles, only to discover that they were not pebbles at all, but shells; the fossilized shells of tiny sea creatures that had lived and died in an ocean immeasurably old. He almost fancied that he could get the scent of it, and at once admonished himself for being a fool. Nevertheless, he popped a few shells into his shirt pocket as a reminder of this experience, assuming that he came through it.

Yet there was a smell, but it was a smell not of an ancient sea. It was an odour of oil and sweat, sharp and acrid on the night air. He sniffed, then shook his head in self-reproach, telling himself that he was imagining things, that he was in danger of cracking up and that it was time to get moving again.

A hand, wiry and incredibly strong, clamped itself over his mouth, stifling all sound. An arm crushed his neck like a vice, strangling him. For the first time in his life, Kalinski knew real, petrifying fear, a terror that would not have allowed him to cry out, even had he been able to do so.

Other hands were moving lightly over his body, touching him from his boots to the top of his head. He felt his revolver being deftly removed. His flesh crawled and successive waves of heat and cold shuddered through him. He felt his senses slipping away. Then, miraculously, the pressure around his neck slackened and he was able to gulp air into his tortured lungs.

He was vaguely aware of muted voices, of whispered

words in a strange language. His battered senses registered the fact that it was not German or Italian; neither was it any form of Arabic known to him. There was no time for conjecture, because he felt the cold, hard shock of a knife blade against his throat, and at the same moment strong hands seized his arms, propelling him forward. He stumbled and a hand gripped his collar, jerking him upright. His fear had now given way to a helpless rage. He toyed with the idea of making a break, but deep down he knew that he would get no more than a few yards before his silent assailants cut him down. They were not going to kill him, at least not yet, so he judged it more prudent to wait and see what happened.

They had not gone more than a couple of hundred yards when the grip on his collar tightened, dragging him to a halt. One of his captors hissed out a word and a response came out of the darkness almost immediately. Kalinski could make out a couple of vehicles, parked in the lee of a low dune.

A figure came towards him out of the darkness. It spoke.

"Well, now, what have we here?" it said, in the unmistakeable tones of upper-class England.

Eleven

Saturday, 23 August 1941. The Libyan Desert

Kalinski leaned against the bonnet of the Chevrolet thirteen-hundredweight truck and surveyed the approaching dawn. The metal of the bonnet was cool to the touch; before long, one would be able to fry an egg on it.

A little soldier appeared in front of him, bearing a mug of steaming tea and a bully beef sandwich. He accepted both gratefully, nodding his thanks. He knew, now, who had captured him so efficiently during the night, and shuddered to think what might have happened, his eyes straying to the hilt of the deadly *kukri* that hung at the Gurkha's belt.

The two Chevrolets were painted a dull pink, a colour that provided excellent camouflage against the backdrop of the desert. Kalinski was aware that the vchicles belonged to a rather swashbuckling outfit called the Long Range Desert Group, a unit that specialised in causing mayhem behind the enemy lines. It had been in existence for less than a year, and its exploits were already legendary.

This particular LRDG patrol was commanded by a young lieutenant called Barrington. He had given

Kalinski a thorough grilling during the night, and was now completely satisfied that the Polish officer was genuine. Kalinski learned that the patrol actually consisted of five Chevrolets and eighteen men; Barrington, having sighted the smoke of the wrecked Italian fighter, had set out with these two to investigate, halting with the onset of darkness. The other trucks were a few miles away, laagered at a spot that was no more than a map reference.

Over breakfast, Barrington told Kalinski something of the LRDG's operations.

"We've found that a five-truck patrol is about the right size," the young officer said. "In the early days a patrol used to consist of eleven trucks, all armed to the teeth – we even carried a 37mm Bofors gun – and about thirty men, but it was far too unwieldy. Too difficult to keep together in the confusion of a raid, and much too easy to spot from the air. The trucks will carry up to two tons, which in practice means that they can accommodate up to three weeks' rations and water, as well as the men and weapons. They'll go for eleven hundred miles without refuelling, and to help us along we've got supplies of fuel stashed away at various cairns around the desert."

Kalinski, for whom this was new territory, was impressed by the thoroughness with which the LRDG had set up its chain of bases in the heart of the desert in just a few months, and said so.

Barrington drank the last of his tea and scrubbed out his mug with a handful of sand.

"Well, it didn't happen overnight," he explained. "Luckily, we had an enormous amount of experience to draw upon. As long ago as 1915, special Light Car Patrols were formed to deal with a chap called Sayed Ahmed es Sherif, a Senussi leader who'd joined forces with the Turks and who was making a thorough bloody nuisance of himself. The Light Car Patrol chaps became expert at driving through the desert and punching Ahmed on the nose before vanishing again. They perfected a lot of the techniques we use now." He smiled suddenly. "Funny thing – we sometimes come across their tyre tracks, even after all this time. They used Model T Fords with three-and-a-half-inch tyres. We use ten-inch balloon tyres, and still get bogged down from time to time. God knows how they managed."

"Are your men all volunteers?" Kalinski asked, as the small force got ready to move out.

"Oh, Good Lord, yes," Barrington said. "Wouldn't have it any other way. Except for the Gurkhas, that is – we've got half a dozen of 'em, attached to us so that they can gain experience of operating behind enemy lines. They are very good at moving around silently, as you doubtless discovered last night."

Kalinski, whose neck still hurt, gave a wry smile.

"These chaps are actually from the 2/7th Gurkha Rifles," Barrington explained, "which is part of the 4th Indian Division. As for the others, they're mostly New Zealanders. Got to watch your step with them, if you're an officer. They don't allow you to make mistakes. What you've got to realise is that this is a pretty exclusive club and that competition to join is fierce. Most of the chaps have had to drop at least one rank to get in. Green and Boulter" – he indicated the driver and signalman of the lead truck – "were both sergeants in the Divisional Cavalry; they dropped to private to join the LRDG, but as you see they've since worked their way up again. They're bloody good scroungers, too. One has to be, at times."

Barrington gave a sudden chuckle. "We had many a laugh in the early days – and many a frustration, too, when we were trying to get hold of the equipment we needed. We caused fits among the Staff types at GHQ with some of our requests. I remember once we slapped in a chit for an Arab shopkeeper's entire stock of bicycle clips, because we didn't have any other kind of clips to fasten our maps to map-boards. Then we indented for a couple of dozen theodolites, and that caused an uproar. Why the hell did we want theodolites, they wanted to know. For accurate navigation across the desert, we told them. A Staff major told us that he'd done a twenty-mile march across the desert using a prismatic compass and that he had only been four hundred yards out at the end of it; when we said that he'd have been five miles out at the end of a four-hundred-mile leg, he began to see the point."

Barrington laughed again. "I won't bother to tell you what happened when we requested two hundred Arab head-dresses," he said. "Suffice to say that we ended up scrounging most of the stuff we needed. We nicknamed the Staff the Short Range Desert Group, because most of 'em can't see farther than the ends of their noses."

The men made space for Kalinski in the lead truck and the two vehicles set off on a southerly heading. Barrington explained that they would make rendezvous with the other three en route and then push southwards to the edge of the Great Sand Sea, their ultimate destination being Siwa Oasis, the LRDG's forward operating base.

"So it looks as though you'll be stuck with us for a few days," Barrington grinned. "As a matter of fact, you were lucky to be picked up; the only reason we were in the area at all was that we were doing a recce of Gambut aerodrome. We'll probably take a look at Maddalena on the way home, too. It's only sixty miles away."

Kalinski was soon to learn that conditions in the southern desert were far different to those of the coastal strip, which was a torment of blistering heat by day and freezing cold by night. There, the climate was made even more unbearable by the powdery sand, churned up by wheels and tracks, that got into every human and mechanical crevice, and by the swarms of bloated flies whose loathsome presence was universal between dawn and dusk.

Here, farther south, on the edge of the great wilderness that stretched across the heart of North Africa, it was different. Here the flies were absent, and the desert itself was clean and unruffled, uncontaminated by the filth of mankind. There was beauty here, too, when the sun was low and casting its shadows across the dunes. Then, early in the morning and at the approach of night, a man could forget for a brief spell the heat of the day, and with his belly full, relax amid the shadows and contemplate that once, an aeon ago, these sands had been fertile and populated by the wandering hunters of ostrich and antelope; and that now, if he were to venture only a few hundred yards away from the well-worn track, his feet would make their imprint on ground that had probably last been trodden 5,000 years ago.

The trucks, all five of them now, made good time over the gravelly desert that lay between the coastal strip and the Sand Sea, and in mid-afternoon they halted in a depression while Barrington detached one of the trucks to take a look at Maddalena. It returned a few hours later and its crew reported that it was occupied by about twenty Italian bombers. Apart from that, there was no sign of activity.

"Well, we'll pop over tonight and tickle 'em up a bit," Barrington said mildly. "Briefing at eighteen hundred."

The moon was rising as they set out for their objective, the trucks scurrying across the desert in arrowhead formation. After a while they picked up a road and turned onto it, the vehicles dropping into single file and proceeding with dimmed headlights, in the manner of a convoy. After a few miles, as they approached the target area, Barrington ordered the lights to be extinguished completely; the road was clearly visible in the moonlight.

The drove over the crest of a small escarpment, and as they moved down the other side they could see their objective. "Good God," Barrington exclaimed in amazement, "it's lit up like a bloody Christmas tree!"

And so it was. Lights were showing everywhere on the airfield, and it was clear that the Italian garrison were not expecting trouble of any kind, doubtless believing that they were too far south of the battle area for anyone to worry about them. If that was the case, they were about to receive a very rude awakening.

Like a country landowner about to inspect his estate, Barrington drove up to the airfield's main gate, jumped down from the truck and swung aside the pole that lay across it. There was no one on guard duty. Then the trucks were through, the drivers' feet pressed hard down on the accelerator pedals as they raced towards the buildings and the dark silhouettes of aircraft parked nearby. Figures suddenly appeared, running frantically between the buildings, and the machine-gunners on the Chevrolets opened fire, sending them tumbling.

The gunner in Kalinski's truck opened up on a dark shape that looked like a fuel bowser, and after a long burst was rewarded by a balloon of flame that burgeoned up, throwing the airfield into start relief. The trucks now dropped into line astern, the gunners raking the parked aircraft as they raced past. Kalinski, torn between a healthy desire to keep his head well down and an unhealthy one to see what was going on, could see the enemy aircraft clearly now, and to his surprise identified them as SM75 transports. Why, he wondered, would the Italians assemble a transport force at this godforsaken outpost?

Whatever they were planning to do with them, he thought, it wasn't going to happen now. Empty shell cases clattered on the floor of the Chevrolet as the gunner continued firing; several aircraft were already burning. The rearmost Chevrolet detached itself from the line and moved slowly among the aircraft, its occupants jumping down to run from one to the other and plant demolition charges on those which had survived the gunfire.

Sporadic fire was beginning to lance at the trucks

from the aerodrome buildings and a burst of tracer snickered over Kalinski's truck, so close to his head that he felt the hot wind of it. Without being ordered, the driver, Green, swung the wheel and headed flat out towards what looked like some sort of accommodation building; most of the enemy fire was coming from it and the machine-gunners hammered away at it. The trucks swung past the building, the gunners continuing to rake it at point-blank range while those whose hands were free hurled grenades through any window they passed. Then, pursued by wildly inaccurate fire, they raced for the entrance again, leaving the airfield well ablaze behind them. The whole action had lasted only five minutes or so.

The moon and the flames from the burning aircraft made the scene almost as clear as day. They showed up, in stark relief, a squat shape that came trundling through the entrance, heading towards them on a collision course. It was an Italian 75/18 Semovente self-propelled gun, much more dangerous than the M13 medium tank with which most Italian armoured divisions were equipped.

The 75mm gun flashed and a shell blasted over the top of the leading truck, the concussion of its passing almost bursting Kalinski's eardrums. He swallowed hard, and pictured the Italian crew frantically reloading for a second shot. Later, he learned that the Semovente was capable of getting off four rounds a minute.

There was no escape route from the airfield other than the entrance, for the perimeter was surrounded by thick coils of barbed wire and metal stakes; not even a Chevrolet going at full speed could break through a barrier like that. The only alternative was to charge full tilt at the Semovente and try to get past it before it could fire another shot. Machine-gun fire from the trucks bounced uselessly off its thick armoured hide in showers of sparks.

The Semovente now opened up with its 6.5mm machine-gun; tracer, blindingly bright, floated towards the speeding trucks and then crackled viciously around them. There was a loud clang as a bullet struck the bonnet, and Green gave a sudden cry. The truck lurched to one side, bouncing wildly as it struck a rut. Barrington reached out to grab the wheel, but the driver pushed his hand away, shouting that he was all right, and regained control.

They were almost on top of the Semovente, skidding and slewing through what looked – and smelled – like a pile of garbage by the roadside, when the Italian's 75mm gun fired again, its barrel at maximum depression. The shell missed the right-hand side of Kalinski's truck by inches and exploded in the one behind, killing its occupants outright.

Green swung the wheel again and Kalinski's truck came alongside the Semovente.

"Everybody out!" Barrington yelled. They did as they were told, Boulter and the gunner assisting Green out of the driving seat, into the back of the truck and over the tailboard. Kalinski risked a look back as they ran clear of the truck and saw Barrington standing precariously on the Semovente's engine casing, holding what looked like an upturned petrol can. A few moments later he tossed the can aside, wedged a Mills bomb against the casing and pulled the pin, jumping down and running for his life.

Four seconds later there was a loud crack as the grenade exploded, followed almost immediately by a roar and a thud that lifted Kalinski and the others – who had thrown themselves to the ground – a good foot into the air and then flung them down again with a blow that knocked the wind from them. With a second mighty concussion the Semovente's ammunition went up, ripping the vehicle apart in a storm of jagged metal that also demolished Barrington's Chevrolet. The men cowered on the ground and waited for the din to subside. White-hot metal fragments and spent bullets spattered the area, and the whole world seemed to reverberate with the thunderclaps of the multiple explosions.

Barrington emerged from the cloud of dust and smoke, reeking of petrol.

"That was close," he said, his voice sounding dully in their sound-battered ears. "How's Green?"

The driver, it turned out, had been lucky. The ricocheting bullet had ripped a groove through the flesh of his upper arm, and although the wound was bleeding profusely it looked much worse than it really was.

They ran back to the wrecked Chevrolet, which was now lying on its side, and retrieved their weapons from it before hurrying to what was left of the second truck. The crew of one of the other vehicles were already there; its commander, a sergeant called Driscoll, shook his head slowly, and a glance inside the mangled remains of the truck told the full and horrific story.

Hurriedly, for the airfield garrison would soon be in

hot pursuit, Barrington gathered his men around him and issued his orders. "Charles, you and the others salvage whatever you can out of that" – he waved a hand at the shattered Chevrolet – "and load it into the others. Get moving – we haven't much time."

Extracting the weapons and provisions – those at any rate that had survived the blast of the 75mm shell – from among the pulped and fragmented bodies in the truck was a far from pleasant task, but it was quickly over. Barrington, Kalinski and the crew of the now defunct lead truck distributed themselves amongst the other three vehicles, Kalinski clambering into Driscoll's. The Pole now found himself armed with a tommy-gun, which someone had thrust into his hands.

The trucks were beginning to come under fire now, and Barrington lost no more time in getting the three surviving vehicles clear of the airfield. They drove off past the Semovente, from whose red-hot hulk there came the nauseating stench of roasting flesh, and sped out through the main entrance. The sounds of pursuit were growing louder now, and silhouetted against the red glow from the aerodrome they could see a number of vehicles, coming up fast.

"They're CV3/35s," Driscoll shouted. "Roughly the equivalent of our Bren gun carrier. Step on the gas," he ordered his driver.

The Italian vehicles were firing with their 8mm machine guns. The Chevrolet gunners were shooting back, and Kalinski saw that the gunner of the rearmost truck, which was armed with a captured Italian 20mm Breda cannon, was right on target. His shells churned up the desert in front of the leading CV3 and then crept up to hit the target at the base of its small turret. The 20mm projectiles pierced the 14mm armour and probably killed the CV3's driver, for the vehicle spun into a series of crazy gyrations that came to an abrupt end when it overturned. The other CV3s continued to follow the trucks for a while, but were soon outdistanced and fell behind, eventually disappearing from view.

The Chevrolets drove on through what was left of the night, heading south and following the Libyan side of the border with Egypt. The whole border area as far south as Giarabub, a large depression that had once been a lake, had been heavily mined, and the only safe way to cross was by way of the northern fringes of the Sand Sea. Until then, the retreating trucks would be vulnerable to air attack – not so likely this far south, but possible.

Shortly after dawn, the possibility turned into reality. The trucks had halted to allow the crews to stretch their legs and have a much-needed 'brew up' when a soldier on lookout duty raised the alarm. Approaching from the north came an aircraft, methodically swinging to left and right as its crew searched for signs of life on the ground. Barrington came up and handed his binoculars to Kalinski, who was munching a tinned sausage with relish.

"What do you make of that?"

Kalinski looked. The approaching aircraft was a low-wing, twin-engine machine with a fixed undercarriage.

"It's a Caproni light bomber," the Pole said. "I have a feeling he's picked up our tracks. All he has to do is follow them until they stop, and he's got us."

Kalinski's reading of the situation proved to be correct. The Italian aircraft curved round to the east, placing the rising sun behind him, then suddenly steadied his machine and headed directly towards the trucks. There was no doubt that he had spotted them, for his bomb doors were open.

The Caproni sped towards them at 500 feet, the roar of its engines swelling. The Breda cannon, which had a longer range than the other weapons, was the first to open fire; its tracers seemed to surround the head-on profile of the Caproni but the bomber came on unchecked. The Vickers and Lewis gunners were now blazing away too, and Kalinski felt certain that some hits must be registering on the aircraft, but the Italian pilot had plenty of guts and he never swerved from his course.

A cluster of small bombs fell from the Caproni's belly and curved down towards the trucks as the bomber's dark shape flashed low overhead. The LRDG men went on firing until the last possible moment, then threw themselves into the scant cover available – among the provisions in the backs of the trucks, or on the sand underneath the vehicles.

Half a dozen explosions cracked out in rapid succession. Kalinski had expected them to be louder, and felt relief. Pissy little bombs, he told himself. Just pissy little bombs. Thank God.

Cautiously, he raised his head. The trucks were veiled by a cloud of drifting dust, kicked up by the explosions. Through it he heard Barrington's cultured voice, asking if anyone was heart. There was a momentary silence, then a laconic New Zealand voice answered him.

"Yeah, my arse is sore. I just dropped the world's biggest turd."

No one, it seemed, had been injured in the air attack; the bombs had embedded themselves in the sandy ground and this had effectively cushioned the blast. The coarse joke helped release the tension and someone laughed, just a little too loudly.

"All right," Barrington shouted, "it's not over yet. Here he comes again!"

This time, the Italian pilot flew broadside on to the trucks, allowing his gunner to rake them with fire from the turret on top of the fuselage. The storm of return fire proved too much for the Italians, however, who decided to call it a day. The Caproni droned away towards the north-west after its second run, apparently unscathed.

After salvaging what they could of their ruined breakfast, Barrington and his men continued on their way, moving steadily southward, following the desert track that led to Giarabub. There was only one route from the gravel depression of Giarabub to the desert plateau that marked the fringe of the Great Sand Sea; it had been discovered by a Major Clayton, one of the founder members of the LRDG, who had located it while working for the Egyptian Government Survey in 1932. He had named the pass 'Easy Ascent', but it was easy no longer; the passage of many vehicles had since churned up the sandy slopes, and negotiating them required a great deal of care. Nevertheless, by the day's end all three trucks had made it safely to the top.

They were entering the country of the dunes now. Ahead of them, as far as the eye could see, great barriers of sand lay astride their path. The dunes ran north-west to south-east, like frozen breakers, scourged by the winds of countless centuries, and when the sun was at its height, casting no shadow, they were invisible.

Despite the fading light Barrington decided to press on for a while. Even with the friendly track gone, they were able to see the way ahead fairly clearly, for the setting sun threw appreciable shadows, revealing where the dunes lay.

The driver of Driscoll's truck was an old hand at the dune-riding game. Kalinski, who was learning fast, noticed that he tried, wherever possible, to keep to ribbed patches of sand that were the colour of butter; these were generally the firm parts. Approaching a dune, he changed down into second gear, and once on the slope kept the truck moving at all cost, for to stop was to risk sinking axle-deep. Meticulously, the drivers of the other trucks stuck to the lead vehicle's wheel tracks.

Once, they were confronted by a dune that was at least 400 feet in height. The driver's technique was to pick a low point in the crest and charge it at speed, changing to first gear as the Chevrolet reached the top and allowing the vehicle to teeter slowly over the edge. This manoeuvre was followed by an exhilarating toboggan-style slide to the bottom of the steepest part of the slope on the other side, a bow-wave of sand spraying out on either side of the truck. Then, as the slope levelled out, he cautiously completed the descent in a zig-zag pattern, so that if he hit a soft patch of sand he could turn into it and slide through.

As the last rays of the sun faded beyond the western line of the dunes, which were now giving way to limestone patches, Barrington halted the group near a small cairn, placed there many years earlier by some forgotten survey party, to make camp. It was growing very cold now, and Kalinski, clad only in shirt and shorts, was grateful for the heavy blanket which one of the men gave him. He pulled it round his shoulders as he ate his evening meal, which consisted of hot bully stew cooked over a desert fire – made by pouring a little petrol into a can filled with sand – and tea, laced with a tot of rum per man. After they had eaten, the men filled their water bottles from the tank carried on each truck in readiness for the following day. Driscoll produced a thermos flask and handed it to Kalinski with the words, "Put your water in that and leave it open during the night. Then you'll have a cool drink tomorrow."

Each man was allowed six pints of water per day. Of these, one was used in the morning brew-up, one was taken with lime juice at midday, two were brewed up with the evening tea, and two more were carried in the water bottle to be drunk sparingly throughout the day. Each man had his own way of eking out the ration; most preferred to restrict themselves to small sips, drinking the remainder at the start of the evening halt. It gave them something to look forward to, and it meant that they could drink their tea at supper-time slowly and with relish instead of using it merely to slake their thirst.

Kalinski slept well that night; perhaps better, he

thought later, than he had ever slept in his life before. He was awakened before dawn by the sounds of the duty cooks getting breakfast ready – it was a chore that everyone shared in turn, officers and men alike – and clasped his hands behind his neck, turning his face to the east to watch the sun rise as quickly as it had set, in a glory of green and gold. This, Barrington told him later, was the best part of the day on a desert patrol – the blissful five minutes with nothing to do before the bellow of 'come and get it' shook away the last vestiges of sleep and spurred everyone from his sleeping bag.

After breakfast – porridge and tinned bacon, the porridge enlivened by a generous shot of whiskey to held dispel the chill of the night – they were soon on the move again, heading across the north-east corner of the Sand Sea. They drove on all day, stopping frequently to unstick vehicles and to allow sun shots to be taken – a tricky business as the sun climbed higher and its shadow grew correspondingly shorter. With the sun at its zenith they halted for a while longer and ate a sparse lunch. No one was very hungry, and Kalinski was grateful for Driscoll's earlier advice about the thermos; the water was still cool, and the addition of some lime juice made it very refreshing.

Later in the day the dunes became lower and more undulating, and as a result the going was easier. After a while the dunes themselves gave way to a plain of black gravel. Kalinski sensed a general rising of spirits, and realised that they would soon be within striking distance of their destination. Darkness fell but Barrington decided to press on, using astro-navigation to set his course. The night was well advanced when they reached a spot called Big Cairn; the mound was only five feet high, but it was the only feature in that flat expanse of plain and was visible from miles away, even in the moonlight.

For some time now, they had been travelling parallel with a huge barbed-wire fence, about six feet high.

"That's the border," Barrington explained to Kalinski. "It runs for two hundred miles and it was erected on the orders of the Italian General Graziani in a bid to stop illegal cross-border activity by the Arabs. It didn't work, of course. They cut gaps in it at various points, but none big enough to allow vehicles to pass through, unfortunately. It ends soon, and we go round it. Then it's a straight run to Siwa, and boy, could I do with a bath!"

The next day, not long after rounding the fence – which ended abruptly in the middle of nowhere, a wasteful and pointless desert Maginot Line – the LRDG force encountered a desert storm. It lay across the southern horizon, a sinister brown line, and grew rapidly larger.

"Not often we run into one down here," Driscoll shouted over the noise of the truck's engine. "Don't worry – they're never anything like as bad as the sandstorms up north."

The sand reached them a few minutes later, flung across the surface of the desert by the *Quibli*, the hot wind from the south. Driscoll was right; the sandstorms of the north were often nightmare walls of dust that rose to a height of hundreds of feet in an impenetrable mass that blotted out everything and brought all movement to a standstill. By comparison, this one was mild and almost tolerable. The grains of sand, scurrying before a forty-mile-an-hour wind, stung the exposed parts of the body, but they did not rise more than twenty feet above the surface and they failed to obscure the sun. The three vehicles carried on, their pace virtually unchecked, and by the time they reached the cairn the storm had blown itself out.

In the evening they descended into Siwa, with its aquamarine pools, its shade, its real beds. Siwa, where Alexander, after wresting control of Egypt from the Persians in 332 BC, had consulted the Oracle of Amon to learn whether he was descended from the gods, and had been answered in the affirmative.

Siwa, where Stanislaw Kalinski, reflecting upon his recent experiences, conceived the germ of an idea which, before long, would prove extremely troublesome to one Erwin Rommel.

Twelve

Gambut Airfield, Wednesday,
twenty-four September 1941. Evening.

*H*auptmann Eduard Neumann – known universally as 'Edu' to his fellow fighter pilots – stared thoughtfully into the eastern sky, towards the Egyptian frontier, and frowned. There was no sign of the returning Messerschmitts, which had set out some time earlier on an offensive patrol, and Neumann was worried.

Maybe he'd been too hard on young Marseille. After all, the lad had gone off by himself that morning and shot down a Martin Maryland reconnaissance aircraft, which was exactly what Rommel wanted the German fighter pilots to do. Keep the enemy's eyes blinded, he had told them, so they have no inkling of our intentions.

"You are only alive," Neuman had told *Leutnant* Hans-Joachim Marseille only a few hours ago, "because you have more luck than common sense. But don't imagine that it will continue indefinitely. One can overstrain one's luck like one can an aeroplane. You have the makings of a top-notch pilot, but to become one you need time, maturity and experience – certainly more time than you have left if you go on as you have been doing."

Neumann had first met Marseille late in 1940, when the younger officer had been assigned to the third *Staffel* of *Jagdgeschwader* 27 at Doberitz. Neumann, who had been *Staffel* commander at the time, had regarded the newcomer with some misgivings right from the outset. Although the 21-year-old Marseille had been a fighter pilot since the autumn of 1940, and although his combat record showed that he had shot down eight British fighters in the English Channel area, he had not risen above the rank of Officer Cadet, when he should have been a *Leutnant* long ago.

He held that rank now, of course, but the reasons behind his slow promotion were not hard to find. They were all there, in Marseille's personal dossier; comments such as 'showed bravado and played practical jokes while under training' and 'committed offences in contravention of flying regulations' appeared over and over again. There was even an entry, underlined in red by one furious instructor, that labelled him a 'flying obscenity'. He could hardly have acquired a worse reputation; all in all, it was a miracle that he had not been thrown out of the *Luftwaffe*. Perhaps, thought Neumann, Marseille's ready wit and personal charm – the gifts of a born Berliner, although Marseille's name betrayed his family's Huguenot origins – had combined to save his neck.

There was no doubt, either, that the beginnings of Marseille's operational career had been decidedly shaky.

His victories over the Channel had been achieved only at the cost of six Messerschmitts, for that was the number of aircraft that had been shot from under him by the RAF. It was a rate of attrition that was hardly calculated to win the war for Germany.

In April 1941 elements of JG 27 were transferred to North Africa, and Marseille managed to get himself into a scrape on the ferry flight from Tripoli to Gazala. His Me 109 developed engine trouble and he was forced to come down in the desert 500 miles short of his destination. Undeterred, he hitched a ride on an Italian truck, eventually arriving at a supply depot. He at once reported to the commanding officer, a general, and passed himself off as a flight commander, explaining that he had to reach his base without delay. The general, whose name was Hellmann, was by no means taken in, but he liked the young man's spirit and obligingly placed his car – an Opel Admiral – at the young airman's disposal.

"You can repay me by getting fifty victories," he told Marseille, who promised to do his best. The following day Marseille arrived at Gazala in style – only a couple of hours after the other Messerschmitts, which had stopped at Benghazi for the night.

A few days after the *Geschwader* settled in at Gazala Marseille destroyed his first aircraft of the North African campaign, but in subsequent battles his eagerness was almost his undoing. Time after time, regardless of personal danger, he would dive straight into the middle of a British formation, with the result that he often returned to base with his aircraft full of bullet holes –

thirty, on one occasion. On another occasion, during a dogfight, he leaned forward in the cockpit – and a burst of machine-gun bullets ripped the back of his helmet. In another dogfight near Tobruk his 109 was badly hit and he had to make a forced landing on no man's land, but he managed to reach the German lines safely.

He will either kill himself, Neumann thought, or he will become a star. The Star of Africa. Already, he had nineteen victories, the last of which was the Maryland. It was only a few days since JG 27 had moved from Gazala to Gambut; rumour had it that the move had been ordered by Rommel himself, who wished to have the strong German fighter contingent closer to his headquarters.

"There they are, sir!" The call came from an orderly, a signals clerk who had just emerged from the headquarters tent, outside which Neumann was standing. Neumann spotted the two Messerschmitts almost in the same instant, curving down towards the airfield: Marseille and his wingman, *Feldwebel* Rainer Pottger. Neumann watched the two aircraft taxy in; the pilots shut down their engines and strolled towards the headquarters tent, lighting cigarettes as they went.

"Any luck, Jochen?" Neumann asked, using Marseille's nickname. The pilot grinned at him disarmingly.

"Just three Hurricanes," he said, blowing out a cloud of smoke.

"Three?" Neumann raised an eyebrow and looked at Pottger, as though seeking confirmation.

"It was incredible, *Herr Major*. Fantastic. I have never seen such tactics. The Tommies – there were five of them

– formed a defensive circle and the *Herr Leutnant* simply dropped into the middle of it. He kept his airspeed low, out-turned the Hurricanes, and fired in short bursts. I had my work cut out keeping track of his victories, noting the times and positions, and protecting his tail. Each time he fired I saw his shells strike first the enemy's nose, then travel along to the cockpit. No ammunition was wasted."

"And there you have it," Marseille said, in a voice that seemed mildly amused. "It's a good thing Rainer here has an eye for detail, don't you think?"

Because of Marseille's exploit the German pilots were in celebratory mood, and Neumann let them have their head that evening. It didn't do any harm once in a while. From their billets on the other side of the airfield the Italians could hear their Allies singing.

"Just listen to them, Tagliotti," Umberto Ricci said. "It's as well they have something to sing about. Glory boys, cruising off over the frontier in their nice new 109Fs while we do all the dirty work. No flak for them," he added morosely.

Tenente Tagliotti glanced sideways at his squadron commander. A profound change seemed to have come over Ricci since the arrival of the German fighters. He had to admit that Ricci's words were true, though; the Germans had completely seized the initiative from their Italian counterparts, leaving them to escort the bombers that continued to attack Tobruk while they, the Germans, carried out daily fighter sweeps over the front line, sometimes venturing as far east as Sidi Barani.

"Well," he said consolingly, "at least we no longer have British fighters to contend with. It's nearly a month now since we saw one over Tobruk, which means they haven't chosen to send in any replacements. I think we are beating them. I think that the big push will come soon, and that we shall have victory at last."

Ricci said nothing. He had seen secret reports that seemed to indicate to him that victory was far from certain. He knew, for example, that from June to September the Italians and Germans had lost 270,000 tons of shipping in the Mediterranean, a situation which the Italian General Staff regarded as catastrophic. As long as Malta remained in British hands, the position could only become worse, and as yet there was no sign of the *Luftwaffe* returning to Sicily to resume its offensive against that troublesome island.

Even the Italian Navy, its resources sadly depleted since the disaster at Taranto, had tried to destroy at least part of Malta's offensive capability. On the night of 25/26 July, the Italian 10th MTB Flotilla had made a gallant attempt to penetrate Grand Harbour and attack some merchantmen while they were still unloading. The frigate *Diana*, with eight explosive boats and two MTBs carrying human torpedo teams, reached Malta, but their approach had been detected by radar and the defences were alerted. One human torpedo team and two explosive boats wrecked the harbour boom but this was to the defenders' advantage, because the explosion caused the St Elmo bridge to collapse and barred the way to the other six explosive boats, which were then destroyed by shore batteries. The two MTBs were also sunk the next morning by fighter-bombers.

Between 8 and 14 September the British aircraft carriers *Ark Royal* and *Furious* had flown off a further fifty-five Hurricanes to Malta. Now, on the 24th, the British Admiralty was mounting a large resupply operation code-named *Halberd*. This involved the passage to Malta of nine large merchantmen, laden with the most urgently-needed supplies and escorted by Force H, heavily reinforced by warships of the Home Fleet, while Admiral Cunningham staged a diversion in the eastern Mediterranean.

The Italian main battle fleet put to sea, together with a strong force of submarines, but air reconnaissance had greatly underestimated the strength of the British force and the Italian surface vessels made no attempt to attack. On the evening of 27 September, when the convoy reached the narrows between Sicily and Tunisia, Force H turned back and the convoy sailed on to Malta escorted by five cruisers and nine destroyers, losing one transport to an aerial torpedo attack. The remainder reached the island safely, bringing the total of merchantmen getting through to Malta since the beginning of the year to thirty-nine. The Royal Navy suffered one casualty in this operation; the battleship *Nelson* was torpedoed by an Italian aircraft south of Sardinia, but reached Gibraltar without further incident. The operation succeeded in delivering 50,000 tons of stores to Malta, providing the island with enough supplies to hold out until May 1942.

These events, of course, were still in the immediate future, and Ricci and his fellow pilots could have no knowledge of them. It was already clear to Ricci, however, that a great crisis of the Mediterranean war was at hand. He was no general, and even less a strategist; it seemed to him, though, that whichever side went on the offensive first was likely to gain the upper hand, and as yet there was no sign of the Axis forces taking the initiative. The latter, in fact, stretched all the way from the frontier back to the mountainous Jebel Akhdar. One Italian division supported by German units manned the frontier defences, two German *Panzer* and three Italian divisions were tied up at Tobruk, and in the Jebel Akhdar were one armoured and two motorised Italian divisions.

Umberto Ricci was not alone in holding such an opinion. It was shared by no less a person than General Sir Claude Auchinleck, who had replaced General Wavell as the British Commander-in-Chief, Middle East, earlier that summer.

Known universally as 'The Auk', Auchinleck was an Indian Army officer who enjoyed a high reputation; a man of fifty-five, tall and broad-shouldered, with crisp lightish-brown hair and a determined chin, an imposing figure with an affable smile and manner that endeared him to all who served under him. He had been commander at Narvik during the ill-fated Norwegian campaign, and after an appointment as General Officer Commanding V Corps and Southern Command in Britain, during the dangerous months when invasion threatened, he had gone back to India in January 1941 as Commander-in-Chief. Six months later, he was summoned by Prime Minister Winston Churchill to take command in the Middle East.

The urgency of the task facing the new C-in-C was underlined in a telegram to him from Churchill, dated 1 July 1941.

"You take up your command at a period of crisis. After all the facts have been laid before you it will be for you to decide whether to renew the offensive in the Western Desert and if so when. You should have regard to the situation in Tobruk and the process of enemy reinforcements in Libya and temporary German preoccupation in the invasion of Russia. You would also consider vexatious dangers of operations in Syria flagging and need for a decision on one or both fronts. You will decide whether and how these operations can be fitted together. The urgency of these issues will naturally impress themselves upon you . . ."

By September the fighting in Syria was over, and Auchinleck had only the Western Desert front to consider. Having weighed up the situation, he established Headquarters, Eighth Army – the successor to the old Western Desert Force – and gave command of the latter to General Sir Alan Cunningham, who had recently completed a highly successful campaign in Italian East Africa.

The Eighth Army was to comprise XIII and XXX Corps, the 29th Indian Brigade Group and the Tobruk garrison. Its task, in the planned offensive operations that were to take place a few weeks later, was to capture Cyrenaica, and to achieve this objective Rommel's armour first had to be destroyed. Once this had been accomplished, Tobruk could be relieved and the whole of Cyrenaica could to retaken. To this end, General

Cunningham was instructed to examine two plans, the first involving a westward advance through Jalo to Benghazi, severing the enemy's supply lines, and the second an advance with the main force directly on Tobruk, with feint attacks along the southern route. Cunningham discarded the first plan. For one thing, the capture of Rommel's main base at Benghazi did not necessarily mean the demise of Rommel's armoured force, as he had fuel and ammunition dumps in place at various other strategic points; for another, it was a long way to Beghazi, and the Eighth Army's own supply line would be vulnerable to flank attacks.

The second plan, the direct advance on Tobruk, was much more viable. In this case, Rommel would be forced to fight, for possession of Tobruk was a key element in his plans.

Much would depend on XXX Corps, under Lieutenant General Willoughby Norrie. Comprising the 7th Armoured Division, the 4th Armoured Brigade, the 1st South African Division and the 22nd Guards Brigade, the Corps would cross the frontier between Sidi Omar and Fort Maddalena – where the defences were weak or non-existent – and then, on the same day, drive north-west on Gabr Saleh and engage Rommel's armour. Rommel had 400 tanks; Norrie had 500.

While this thrust was taking place, General Godwin-Austen's XIII Corps – with the New Zealand Division, the 4th Indian Division and the 1st Army Tank Brigade – was to contain the enemy frontier defences between Sidi Omar and the coast, and then envelop them from the south. Afterwards, it would move towards

Tobruk, mopping up enemy resistance between Bardia and Tobruk as it went along.

At Tobruk, the garrison commander, General Scobie, would be instructed to attempt no breakout until the *Panzer* divisions had either been destroyed or rendered incapable of interfering. When the breakout did take place, the garrison, which would then come under General Norrie's command, would attack and capture a strategic ridge at El Duda, south-east of Tobruk. A second ridge, at Sidi Rezegh, would be taken by XXX Corps. Between these two ridges ran the Axis lifeline to their front-line troops in the east.

Finally, there was Oasis Force. Operating well to the south of the main line of advance, this would comprise the 29th Indian Infantry Brigade Group and the 6th South African Armoured Car Regiment, which would push out from Siwa and cross over 200 nautical miles of desert to occupy Gialo Oasis and protect the airstrip to the north of it, known as Landing Ground 125. The way would be led by a squadron of the Long Range Desert Group. Once established at Gialo, three squadrons of fighters and fighter-bombers would fly into LG 125; from there, they would be able to attack the Axis forces from the rear.

Auchinleck and Cunningham were conscious that to keep the army supplied during the coming war of movement over such a wide and desolate area would tax their administrative resources to the limit. It was estimated that over 30,000 tons of supplies of every kind would be needed during the first week of the offensive alone. The plan, therefore, was to establish three forward bases to support the operation – one near Sidi Barani, one near the railhead at Mis Heifa near the frontier and the third at Giarabub to supply Oasis Force. Six forward maintenance bases were also to be set up, each containing food, ammunition, petrol, water and workshops.

The plan also called for a water pipeline to be extended by 150 miles from Alexandria to the front. Even so, the ration per man per day, for all purposes, could not exceed threequarters of a gallon. That situation would only ease with the relief of Tobruk, when water and other essential supplies could be brought in by ships using the harbour.

The fact that the new British commander was planning something big had not gone unnoticed by the shrewd commander of what was now called *Panzerarmee Afrika*, Erwin Rommel. The general had plans of his own. A visit to Hitler's headquarters in Germany in July, followed by an interview with the Italian dictator Mussolini in Rome in August, had left him supremely confident. Hitler had given permission for the *Luftwaffe* to use its new 2½-ton bombs in support of Rommel's planned assault on Tobruk, and his plans for that assault had been endorsed by Mussolini.

The fresh troops that would carry out the big attack were arriving in numbers, too, spearheaded by an elite force, the 90th Light Division, in August; and almost the whole of his battle staff had changed, too. He had a new operations officer, a tall, aristocratic *Oberstleutnant* of thirty-nine called Siegfried Westphal, a professional soldier to his fingertips, who agreed wholeheartedly when Rommel decided to move his headquarters from the relative comfort of Beda Littoria in the Green Mountains, first to Gazala and then to Gambut – bug-infested, fly-blown and filthy, but midway between Tobruk and the frontier, where the coming decisive battles would be fought.

Here, the Axis force steadily built up their supply dumps and workshops, large, well-camouflaged factories well-equipped with machine tools, heavy lifting gear and huge quantities of spare parts, so that disabled armoured fighting vehicles could be plucked from the battlefield and returned to action within days after being repaired.

The walls of his headquarters were festooned with maps, not just of North Africa, but of the Atlantic and Russia. Every day, he studied the situation on the Russian front, seeing the victorious German forces encircling one Soviet army after another, longing for the day when his own army would be sufficiently strong to launch the final assault on Tobruk.

His plan was straightforward enough. First of all, days of heavy bombing would soften up the garrison's defences. Then, after a massive artillery bombardment, the 90th Light Division would open up a breach in the south-eastern perimeter for the 15th *Panzer* Division to pass through. As the German force pushed straight on to the port, its left flank would be secured by the two divisions of the Italian 21st Corps. He would leave a mobile reserve in the desert, strong enough to deal with any British force that tried to interfere.

And he would secure command of the air. That should not be difficult, now that *Major* Neumann's *Jagdgeschwader* was at the front, with its fine pilots. Pilots like the rising star, a man rapidly growing in fame until he rivalled Rommel himself for space in the German newsreels. Hans-Joachim Marseille.

Thirteen

Sidi Barani, Egypt. Friday, 31 October 1941

"So that's him," Armstrong said. "That's the one who's been causing all the trouble."

He looked again at the face that stared up at him from the front cover of *Signal*, the German Army's propaganda magazine. The journal was crumpled and water-stained; someone had found it washed up on the beach, and had taken the trouble to dry it out. Armstrong was pleased. He liked to know his enemy.

"That's him," Dickie Baird agreed. "Not much to look at, is he? Bit effeminate, I'd say."

To be truthful, Marseille's heart-shaped features, with his high forehead and big, wide-set eyes, did give that impression. There was nothing to indicate that this man was a cold, calculating killer, a master of his profession, with twenty-five victories to his credit.

Baird glanced at his watch. It would be dawn soon, and time for the mission. Armstrong looked at his friend anxiously, conscious that Baird's face looked unusually pale and drawn.

"Are you sure you're going to be all right for this one, Dickie?" he asked.

Baird nodded. "Sure. I'm OK. A bit tired, that's all. A whiff of oxygen will soon put me right. Tell you the truth, I don't think I've felt really well since we were in Tobruk."

Armstrong nodded. Baird had picked up some sort of bug during his time in the fortress, and had yet to make a full recovery. By rights, he should not have been flying at all, but the Desert Air Force was still short of skilled fighter pilots, particularly ones with experience of tactical reconnaissance.

Armstrong realised with something of a shock that it was two months to the day since his squadron's pilots and ground crew, or what was left of them – with no Hurricanes still airworthy and with their airstrip out of action through continual bombing – had been evacuated from Tobruk. It had been a harrowing time, with no word about Kalinski, who had gone missing during the big air engagement of 22 August; it had been several days before the Pole had turned up, safe and well, with an extraordinary tale to tell, bubbling with enthusiasm for a scheme he'd dreamed up while out in the wilderness with the Long Range Desert Group.

It was a good scheme: Armstrong had seen that at once, and had asked Kalinski to draw up a detailed plan. This had been quickly passed up the chain of command to the Air Officer Commanding, Air Marshal Arthur Tedder, who liked it and approved it, as did Generals Cunningham and Auchinleck when it came to their attention.

Armstrong, as a consequence, was now in command of three squadrons, one with Hurricanes and two with Curtiss Kittyhawks. The Hurricane squadron was at Sidi

Barani, the other two back on the Nile, training hard. All three would come together a few days before the start of Auchinleck's planned offensive, ready to move to Landing Ground 125 for operations against the enemy's rear and southern flank.

The forthcoming offensive had now been given a code-name: Operation *Crusader*. It was scheduled to unfold in mid-November. In the meantime, air reconnaissance flights deep into enemy territory were carried out on a daily basis, the aircrews braving terrible risks now that the Messerschmitts were on the prowl.

The last three reconnaissance aircraft had failed to return, which was why Dickie Baird was flying the mission on this October morning. It was his turn, and he had flatly refused to allow anyone else to take his place. He would not be alone; Jackie Weston would be going with him, to cover his tail while he made his low-level photographic runs.

The pilots of the Hurricane squadron, including the replacements, were all experienced in the science of tactical reconnaissance, and had developed techniques of their own to locate enemy positions or vehicles. With the help of all available intelligence, pilots would plot the likely position of the enemy and draw a circle of ten miles radius around it on their maps; they would then carry out an intensive visual reconnaissance of the area inside the circle, often drawing intense anti-aircraft fire in the process.

As the enemy poured more troops into the area immediately behind the front line, ground fire became increasingly dangerous, so the pilots adopted a technique whereby one aircraft would carry out the reconnaissance from an altitude of not less than 6,000 feet, beyond the range of small arms fire and some of the light flak, while a second aircraft would fly a thousand feet higher, its pilot on the lookout for gun flashes. So far, these tactics had worked well, and losses had dropped.

Baird actually enjoyed tactical reconnaissance work, coming into his own when very low flying was involved. Every pilot has a preference for a certain type of flying. Some enjoy the sheer precision of perfect 'circuits and bumps'; others find a heady delight in pushing an aircraft to the limit of its ceiling, to a vantage point miles in the sky from which they can look down on the far horizons, curving away on the edge of a world so remote as to be unreal. For Baird, however, nothing would ever beat flying fast and low for sheer exhilaration. It needed all one's concentration, especially over the terrain of North Africa, where the rock and sand of the desert merged into a hazy, ill-defined horizon and ghostly ripples of heat shimmered and danced, tempting the unwary eye like will-o'-the-wisps.

But Baird, who was primarily a naval pilot, was used to low flying over the sea, which in a sense was not a great deal different.

Now, as he and Weston flashed over the frontier, chased by the fresh colours of the desert sunrise, the old exhilaration came over him, shaking off whatever it was – physical or mental, he had not yet estab-lished to his own satisfaction – had been troubling him. Ignoring the minimum 6,000-foot rule, he stayed down low, intent on achieving the maximum possible element of surprise and so spoiling someone's break-fast.

The Hurricane he was flying was a TacR Mk I, fitted with a cine camera in the port wing and armed with six machine-guns instead of eight. Weston was flying a Hurricane IIB with twelve Browning guns, an armament that could kick up a considerable dust storm and which was effective against soft-skinned targets such as trucks.

The two Hurricanes flew steadily on towards their main objective, the confluence of desert tracks at Bir Hacheim, forty miles south-west of Tobruk, where fresh concentrations of enemy armour were reported to be assembling. The desert appeared empty and lifeless in the contrasting light and shadow of the sunrise, but as he flew on Baird saw plenty of evidence of man's recent presence. Between Bir Hacheim and El Adem, the airfield closer to Tobruk where many of the bombers pounding the fortress were based, the desert was churned by a maze of tracks, twisting and circling and apparently going nowhere, as though some mad ploughman had been at work. There were vehicles, too, dotted here and there, many with blackened areas around them which betrayed the searing heat that had destroyed them. Some were Italian, relics of O'Connor's offensive at the beginning of the year; but others were British, abandoned in the headlong retreat that had followed Rommel's thrust into Cyrenaica.

Baird tensed suddenly, becoming fully alert as he sighted a dust-cloud ahead of him. Half a dozen small dots at its base quickly resolved themselves into trucks, travelling in rough line abreast formation. He called up Weston over the R/T, drawing the other pilot's attention to them. They looked like toys against the immensity of the desert. Baird was unable to identify them, but they must be either German or Italian; he knew from his briefing that there were no LRDG patrols this far north, so there was no chance of any tragic error.

Well, he told himself, this is an armed reconnaissance, so here goes. He ordered Weston to follow him down into the attack and lined up the Hurricane carefully, dropping to a hundred feet. The men in the trucks had seen him coming and the vehicles started to scatter, but they were too late. Baird opened fire at 500 yards and his bullets hurled up a miniature sandstorm around the nearest truck. Tiny figures tumbled over the tailboard and lay motionless. He yawed the aircraft slightly, spraying the remaining vehicles, and kept on firing until the last moment. The trucks flashed beneath him and he went into a shallow climb, looking back. Smoke was rising from two of the vehicles, which appeared to have collided. As he took a last glance, the scene dissolved in a mighty eruption of smoke and sand. That, thought the pilot with satisfaction, was one load of ammunition that wouldn't get to Rommel.

Suddenly, he was concerned for Weston, whose aircraft he could not see. But he need not have worried; a moment later he sighted the other Hurricane, shooting into view through the spreading smoke cloud.

"Christ, leader," Weston said, "did you have to do that?"

Baird chuckled into his oxygen mask and resumed

his original course. A range of hills, extending east and west for about twenty miles and rising to more than 500 feet from the desert floor, appeared directly ahead of the speeding fighters. Beyond the high ground lay the coast road along which the Axis supply convoys were trundling daily towards the front line. The Hurricanes made for the extreme right-hand edge of the hills, flying round it until they picked up the road.

Thirty seconds later, they saw the first group of enemy tanks. There were about thirty of them, a mixture of German Mk IVs and smaller Italian M13s. They were stopped by the side of the road, but their crews were clearly taking no chances. As Baird raced towards them, his camera whirring, smoky lines of tracer converged on his Hurricane and that of Weston, who was flying abreast, a couple of hundred yards away on his right. Weston was firing, his bullets kicking up dust that partially obscured the enemy vehicles.

Baird held his own fire, hunching his body into a ball in the cockpit, fighting the temptation to fling the aircraft away from the danger and forcing himself to hold it steady for the camera run, a difficult enough task because of the eddies of turbulence that came rippling across the road from the hills on the left.

The Hurricane shuddered as bullets struck home, but the engine maintained its healthy roar and the controls stayed firm. Baird stayed low, flashing past the tanks so close that he had a vivid impression of the stark black crosses on their flanks and the dusty figures of the machine-gunners, crouched behind their weapons on the turrets of the armoured monsters. Then the danger was behind him and he gave a sudden gasp, surprised to find that he had been holding his breath.

A glance showed him that Weston had come through unharmed. The other pilot drew closer, and after a few seconds called up over the radio.

"You've collected a few holes in the rear fuselage, leader. No serious damage, though, I don't think."

Baird acknowledged the call briefly, feeling some relief. He knew, though, that the Hurricane was a tough old bird; with her wood-and-fabric structure she could sustain damage that would be fatal to other aircraft, and still fly home.

Some miles further on they encountered more tanks and a convoy of open trucks, but their crews were clustered in small groups some distance away from the vehicles and appeared to be having breakfast. Baird ran some more film, then gave the convoy a lengthy squirt with his Brownings, for good measure. There was no answering fire.

Now for the difficult part, Baird thought, and turned sharply to starboard, hugging the contours of the terrain. His next task was to make a fast run over El Adem, the enemy-occupied airfield that posed a direct threat to Tobruk. It lay directly in front of his nose, about five miles distant. The two Hurricanes, in line astern now, were flying in shadow through a broad pass that cut through a ridge, the roar of their Merlins reverberating from the walls on either side, dislodging small avalanches of stones. Beyond the pass lay the open desert once more, and the airfield.

On a sudden impulse, alerted by some sixth sense,

Baird ordered Weston to climb. He pushed the throttle wide open and pulled back the stick, taking the fighter up in a fast, steep ascent. The Hurricane leapt out of the pass as though hurled from a catapult. Baird was momentarily dazzled as the fighter emerged into the full glare of the swiftly-rising sun. He blinked several times, turning his head aside from the intense light, and pulled down his tinted goggles. Then he glanced at his rear-view mirror as he levelled out, and blinked again.

Positioned squarely in the centre of the mirror, dark and menacing, were the head-on silhouettes of two single-engined aircraft. And they were close, far too close for comfort. Urgently, he alerted Weston over the radio. "Bandits at six o'clock, closing fast. Stand by to break on my order."

After a short pause Weston replied that he had seen them too. Baird, as always happened to him in situations such as this, became icily cool. He calculated that he had several more seconds before the enemy aircraft came within firing range. He could identify them now as Me 109s; this was going to be a tough one. He wriggled in his straps, craning his neck in an attempt to get a better view, careful not to make any sudden control movement; he must not let the other pilots know that he had seen them.

He counted off the seconds, willing himself not to cheat. He had to time his move as precisely as possible. Five . . . four . . . three . . .

"Stand by . . . BREAK!"

He pushed the left rudder pedal hard and pulled the stick over into his left thigh. The Hurricane stood on her wingtip and came round in a hard turn. It was a manoeuvre that Baird had developed during the Norwegian campaign, when the Blackburn Skua dive-bombers of his squadron had come under attack by much speedier German fighters, and it had worked well then.

This time was no exception. The enemy pilot who had been directly behind Baird, closing in on his tail, was taken completely by surprise and overshot, presenting his aircraft to Baird in vivid detail as he skidded past.

It was a Messerschmitt Me 109F, the colour of tawny sand on top, sky blue underneath. It had a white spinner, and a white band around the rear fuselage. On the side of the fuselage, immediately in front of the white-edged black cross, was a large, yellow number 14. For a second Baird glimpsed the enemy pilot, hunched forward in the cockpit.

Black smoke poured from the Messerschmitt's exhaust stubs as the pilot put the engine into boost. The fighter accelerated quickly and began to climb, followed by Baird, who loosed off an ineffectual burst of fire at it. He knew that the Hurricane could not match the Me 109F in a climb, but he also knew that, with its engine in boost configuration, the 109 would be using fuel at an alarming rate.

The enemy fighter was rapidly opening the distance between the two aircraft. Baird, mindful of his task, decided to break off the combat, if he could, and make a fast run over El Adem. He dived away and descended almost to ground level, calling Weston over the R/T as he did so. There was no reply.

He could see the enemy airfield quite clearly now. A couple of aircraft, probably *Stukas*, were in the circuit. A glance in his mirror revealed the Messerschmitt, curving down in pursuit and closing fast. A moment later, flashes lit up its nose and wings as the German pilot opened fire. Tracer flickered over the Hurricane, missing it by only a few feet.

In desperation, Baird loosed off a burst of gunfire into thin air. Grey smoke trails streamed back from his wings and their sudden appearance must have startled the enemy pilot, who abruptly sheered off to the left. The ruse had bought Baird a few seconds of time and he raced across the airfield perimeter, his camera whirring, conscious that the 109 was behind him again.

Then the airfield defences opened up, and almost at once Baird knew that his tactics were working. Experience had taught him that the first bursts of ground fire almost always exploded behind an attacking aircraft flying at low level, and this time was no exception. Glancing back, he saw a string of black tufts blossom out, immediately in the path of his pursuer. The Messerschmitt immediately flicked away and he caught a glimpse of its blue underside as its pilot steep-turned to get clear of the flak.

With the airfield behind him Baird turned away and made for the coast, twenty miles away, still at low level. There was no sign of the pursuing Messerschmitt. Weston was still failing to answer the radio, which was not surprising, because at that moment Baird's fellow pilot was floating down under a parachute, wondering bitterly what life in captivity was going to be like. His first taste of it was not too bad; he landed almost on top of a group of German tanks, whose crews bandaged up his sprained ankle and gave him some coffee before a truck arrived to take him away.

Baird arrived back at Sidi Barani, with his fuel dangerously low, his detour out to sea having consumed more than intended. Shaking like a leaf, he recounted his story to Armstrong, describing everything down to the markings he had observed on his attacker's Messerschmitt. Armstrong frowned, recalling something, and picked up the copy of *Signal* which they had been studying early that morning.

Baird looked again at the colour photograph of Hans-Joachim Marseille. The German pilot was standing in front of a Messerschmitt, only the rear half of which was visible. On the fuselage, clearly visible, was a large yellow fourteen.

Fourteen

Tuesday, 18 November 1941.
Rommel's Headquarters, Gambut.

"The *whole* of Thirty Corps, you say?"
There was a sharp edge to Rommel's voice that made the intelligence officer nervous. It was as though the events now unfolding in the desert were the result of some mistake he had made, personally.

"Yes, sir. The British 7th Armoured Division asppears to be leading the attack, supported by the South African Division. That is General Pienaar's division, *Herr General.*"

Rommel made an impatient gesture. "I know, I know!" He looked at the map in front of him, pondering. Air reconnaissance had shown considerable bodies of enemy troops moving in the desert south of Matruh over the past couple of weeks, but these had been taken for nothing more than large-scale exercises. Rommel had not expected an entire British Army Corps to blast its way through the wire below Fort Maddalena.

"Tank strength?" he asked abruptly.

"We estimate four hundred and fifty, sir. Together with a divisional support group of motorised infantry and artillery."

"So." Rommel thoughtfully tapped the map with the tip of his second finger, a habit of his. The map had recently been updated to show the latest position of the British armoured spearheads. It seemed they were making for the Trigh El Abd, the desert track that ran across Libya to the Egyptian frontier.

What is this, Rommel wondered. A raid in force, to bring us to battle and inflict casualties, or a full-scale offensive? Whatever it is, it has taken us by surprise. To make matters worse, it had forestalled his own planned offensive into Egypt, scheduled to take place in a few days' time.

Leaning forward, he studied the dispositions of his own troops. The position, he thought, was not entirely unfavourable. The 15th *Panzer* Division was on the coast east of Tobruk, preparing for the assault on the fortress; the 21st *Panzer* and the 90th Light Divisions had also been pulled back for the same reason, leaving the Italian 21st Corps and a few German infantry battalions in the front line. From west to east, the perimeter positions were held by the 27th *Brescia*, the 17th *Pavia*, the 102nd *Trento* and the 25th *Bolognia* Divisions. To the south, the 101st *Trieste* Motorised Division was at Bir Hacheim, the 132nd *Ariete* Armoured Division at Bir el Gubi, on the Trigh el Abd, and the *Savona* Infantry Division on the frontier at Sidi Omar. In addition, the Halfaya-Sollum-Bardia defensive position was manned mostly by Italians and by elements of the 164th Infantry Division, which included large numbers of elderly reservists and imperfectly trained recruits.

As the morning wore on, however, the arrival of more

bad news at Rommel's headquarters made the Axis position somewhat less tenable. The British XIII Corps, attacking in the north, had virtually isolated Sollum and Bardia. Intelligence reports indicated that the attack in this sector was spearheaded by New Zealand troops, supported by an Indian division and a tank brigade with about 130 armoured fighting vehicles. The reports also indicated that the New Zealanders were thrusting up the Trigh Capuzzo, the road that led north to join the Via Balbia, the main coast road.

Once on the Via Balbia, the New Zealanders could easily push on towards Gambut, threatening Rommel's headquarters.

"We had better prepare to become mobile," Rommel told his staff, and ordered the Italian 25th *Bologna* Division forward from the eastern perimeter of Tobruk to meet the New Zealand threat.

In the afternoon, reports began to come in that two reconnaissance battalions of the 21st *Panzer* Division under *Oberstleutnant* Baron Irnfried von Wechmar, equipped with armoured cars, had encountered British armour on the Trigh el Abd, and that there had been a brisk fight.

Confused reports continued to reach Rommel, mingled with vague rumours. At 8 p.m. General Ludwig Crüwell, commander of the *Afrika Korps* since Rommel had been promoted to the command of *Panzerarmee Afrika*, telephoned Rommel and sought permission to send a regiment of 15th *Panzer* south to Gabr Saleh, towards which the British attack seemed to be developing, and place the rest of the armoured division on full alert. The call was not made until after much discussion had taken

place between Crüwell and his Chief of Staff, General
Fritz Bayerlein, for Rommel had always dismissed any
notion of a British offensive as absolutely impossible.

Yet here it was; it was happening.

"We must not lose our nerve," Rommel snapped, when
Crüwell phoned him. "You are not to send the *Panzer*
regiment south. It would show our hand too soon. Come
and meet me, and we shall discuss the matter. Noon
tomorrow will do."

"Noon tomorrow!" grated Crüwell, a dour Rhinelander
not given to displays of emotion. "The British will be in
Gambut by then."

Taking matters into his own hands, he told Bayerlein
to place 15th *Panzer* on alert. The whole division must be
ready to move into action during the night, if necessary.
The Italian commander, General Gastone Gambara, also
appreciated the seriousness of the situation, and placed
the *Ariete* and *Trieste* armoured divisions on full alert
at the Bir el Gubi end of the Trigh el Abd.

The night passed quickly, even though it was made
miserable by a torrential storm that had one beneficial
outcome as far as the attackers were concerned; it
made the German airfields unserviceable for much of
the following day. In any case, the weather was not
conducive to flying; the sky was grey and overcast.

At daylight on 19 November, with no sign of the
Luftwaffe and no apparent reaction from the enemy,
General Gott, commanding the 7th Armoured Division,
ordered the 22nd Armoured Brigade to push on to a
point west of Bir el Gubi while 7th Armoured Brigade
headed north towards Sidi Rezegh. The 4th Armoured

Brigade was to protect the right flank of the movement and also the left flank of XIII Corps, when the latter moved up.

The 22nd Armoured Brigade was ill-equipped for the task assigned to it. It had only arrived in Egypt early in October and had no experience of desert warfare; moreover, its Cruiser Mk 6 tanks – called Crusaders, which were armed with a two-pounder main gun and two machine-guns – were prone to mechanical breakdown.

In the ensuing confused battle with the *Ariete* Division, in which the Italians stood their ground gallantly, the British lost forty tanks, more than a quarter of the Brigade's total strength; the Italians lost thirty-four. While this action was being fought, however, the 7th Armoured Brigade raced on to Sidi Rezegh, capturing the airfield there. The British tanks were now only ten miles from the Tobruk perimeter.

Meanwhile, the 4th Armoured Brigade had halted at Gabr Saleh. It was still there in the middle of the afternoon, when, out of clearing skies, relays of *Stukas* appeared and subjected it to a series of blistering attacks that ceased abruptly just before 16.00. The reason was soon clear.

Out of the desert came ninety Mk IV tanks of the 21st *Panzer* Division under the command of *Oberst* Fritz Stephan. By the time they withdrew at nightfall, the 4th Armoured Brigade's strength was down to ninety-eight tanks; it had begun the offensive with 164.

The attack by XIII Corps, meanwhile, had gone well, and at the end of 19 November General Auchinleck felt confident enough to send a signal to Winston Churchill.

'It seems that the enemy was surprised and unaware of the imminence and weight of our blow,' it read. 'Indications, although they have to be confirmed, are that he is now trying to withdraw from the area Bardia-Sollum. Until we know the area reached by our armoured troops today it is not possible to read the battle further at the moment. I myself am happy about the situation . . .'

On the morning of 20 November Rommel still remained unconvinced that the British operation was a serious attempt to lift the siege of Tobruk. Crüwell was convinced, however, and ordered both his *Panzer* leaders to concentrate their divisions at Gabr Saleh. "I refuse," he told them, "to stand idly by and watch the enemy advance unmolested on Tobruk."

That evening, an intelligence officer handed Rommel a translation of part of a news bulletin broadcast by the BBC's Cairo station. 'The Eighth Army,' it said, 'with about 75,000 men excellently armed and equipped, have started a general offensive in the western desert with the aim of destroying the German-Italian forces in Africa.'

"We shall see about that," Rommel said, his jaw set in determination. "We shall see." He stayed up all night, issuing a flurry of orders. First of all, he telephoned Crüwell, emphasised the critical nature of the situation, and ordered the *Afrika Korps* commander to send his two armoured divisions north from Gabr Saleh to Tobruk at first light. Their objective: to recapture the airfield at Sidi Rezegh, where British tanks, artillery and infantry were clearly preparing for a drive towards the Tobruk perimeter.

At 06.30 Rommel himself visited the German artillery that was dug in at Belhamed, some three miles north of the airfield, the artillery that had been pounding Tobruk, and ordered its commander to turn his guns around and lay down a barrage on Sidi Rezegh airfield. Through his binoculars, as the light grew better, he could see the tanks and infantry massing on the landing ground for their advance on Tobruk, whose defenders had begun to drive a salient into the siege lines in readiness to break out. The plan was for the garrison to push through and link up with the airfield force at El Duda, a position only thinly held by German infantry.

Rommel raised his binoculars a few degrees and scanned the southern horizon. A moment later, he smiled jubilantly. A huge dust cloud betrayed the fact that the entire *Afrika Korps* was descending on Sidi Rezegh at full speed.

Around him, the guns were already thundering, battering the airfield, which was soon obscured by clouds of smoke and dust. Some of the British armour was already moving towards Tobruk and Rommel took personal command of the counter-attacks between Belhamed and El Duda, carried out by the armoured cars of von Wechmar's reconnaissance battalion. But it was the 88mm guns that did most of the damage. There were only four of them, but they sent tank after tank up in flames.

On the airfield, all was chaos as the *Panzers* charged the primeter, firing as they came. The flimsy British cruiser tanks scurried and flared and shattered, out-gunned and out-armoured. Many deeds of gallantry went unrecorded in that brief and vicious battle, as British tank commanders charged headlong at the enemy armour in a desperate bid to get within range; but by the end of the morning the 7th Armoured Brigade had only ten tanks left, and for the time being the breakout from Tobruk was doomed.

Rommel was unable to sleep that night. For hour after hour, in his desert headquarters – so far under no direct threat – he pored over his battle maps, examining one option after another. There were indications that another British armoured brigade was moving north, its task to cut the *Afrika Korps'* line of retreat, should this become necessary. That must not be allowed to happen, and it was clear to Rommel that only one immediate course of action was open to him.

That night, as it would do for several nights to come, a black-painted Heinkel 115 floatplane droned in low towards the North African coast. Forty miles east of Tobruk, unseen, it alighted on the sea, taxying into a long inlet. A group of six heavily-armed men scrambled from it, assisted by Lieutenant Hansen's experienced crew, and paddled ashore on a rubber raft, which they buried before proceeding inland. In the days to come they, and other groups like them, would have a vital and dangerous task to perform, monitoring the movement of enemy traffic on the coast road and carrying out acts of sabotage. They were equipped with powerful radio sets, which they would use to bring down the fighter-bombers of the Desert Air Force like a whirlwind on the enemy.

They were the men of the Special Air Service, the brainchild of a young subaltern called David Stirling, who had been its inspiration and driving force right from the start. In 1940, Stirling had transferred from the Scots Guards to No 8 Commando, a newly-formed force under the command of Captain Robert Laycock, and in the autumn of that year it had arrived in the Middle East with two other Commandos totalling 2,000 men. Early in 1941 Laycock's force had been briefed to land on the Greek Island of Rhodes and secure it against an enemy invasion, but this plan had been thwarted by the swift German campaign in Greece and the subsequent capture of Crete. Layforce, as Laycock's organisation was now known, had been split up piecemeal, part of it fighting a desperate rearguard action in Crete, part against the Vichy French in Syria and another part defending a sector of the perimeter in the besieged port of Tobruk.

Word had come down from Cairo that Layforce was to be disbanded, a decision that by no means found favour with its founder and a number of other tough, efficient young officers like David Stirling. They saw Layforce, or a derivative of it, as an ideal means of striking hard at the enemy's lines of communication – which, in the summer of 1941, had grown steadily longer as Rommel's forces plunged eastward through Libya. Stirling and the others felt that small commando groups, operating deep behind the enemy lines, could wreak as much havoc as a couple of divisions. The groups could either be parachuted to their objectives or landed on the coast from small craft or seaplanes.

David Stirling, recovering in hospital from the effects

of a parachute jump that had gone wrong, had made up his mind to try to form a special commando unit for just that purpose. But at that time Stirling was still only a second lieutenant, and he knew that any formal approach would be bound to meet with a blank wall of refusal. So, with characteristic determination, he made up his mind to circumvent the usual channels and take his case direct to General Auchinleck.

By an extraordinary combination of guts and good fortune, the scheme had worked. Bluffing his way into Middle East Command HQ in Cairo, Stirling had secured an interview with Auchinleck's deputy, General Ritchie – or rather, had walked into Ritchie's office unheralded – and presented him with the plan he had carefully drawn up during the long weeks in hospital. Ritchie had been impressed, and had promised to take up the idea with the C-in-C. He kept his word: Stirling was summoned for an interview with 'The Auk', and as a result received authority to form a new commando force built initially around a nucleus of sixty-six officers, NCOs and soldiers drawn from what remained of Layforce.

The new force was called 'L' Detachment of the Special Air Service Brigade. No such brigade existed; the title was designed to fool the enemy into believing that large-scale commando-style operations were soon to be mounted against them. Its headquarters were established at Kabrit, on the shores of the Great Bitter Lake, and training was to be completed by the beginning of November, when 'L' Detachment was to mount its first operation – an attack on five enemy airfields in support of Operation *Crusader*.

The raid, carried out on the night before the offensive started, was a disaster. The commandos were to be dropped near their targets by five Bristol Bombay transport aircraft, but strong winds whipped up a sandstorm, blotting out landmarks, and when the parachutists were dropped they were blown miles from their objectives. Of the sixty men who set out, only twenty-two survived to be picked up at a pre-determined rendezvous by patrols of the Long Range Desert Group. The rest were either killed or captured.

The disaster might have spelled the end of the embryo SAS; instead, General Auchinleck wisely realised that the adverse and unexpected weather conditions had been solely to blame. As far as Stirling and his colleagues were concerned, the failure of the airborne raid had provided a salutary lesson in tactics; parachuting down to objectives was obviously not the ideal answer, and closer co-operation with the Long Range Desert Group seemed to be a better alternative. The LRDG could drop the commandos within marching distance or their targets, and pick them up again afterwards.

Meanwhile, the deployment of small groups to carry out reconnaissance and sabotage along the Via Balbia meant that the SAS had been given a second chance to vindicate itself. Much depended on the events of the next few days, which hopefully would see Rommel booted out of Cyrenaica.

But even as the first SAS parties were crawling into their observation posts, Rommel was taking steps to ensure that no such thing would happen. At 07.00 on Saturday, 22 November, he returned to his vantage point on Belhamed hill to watch his artillery resume its pounding of Sidi Rezegh airfield, still held by the British, and at noon he ordered the commander of 21st *Panzer* Division, General von Ravenstein, to launch an all-out assault. It began at 14.20, when fifty-seven tanks of *Oberst* Stephan's regiment attacked from the west and motorised infantry assaulted from the north.

The British gunners put up a terrific resistance, and died to a man beside the twisted wreckage of their weapons. Towards the end of the afternoon, a dust-cloud in the south heralded the late approach of the 22nd Armoured Brigade, an event that heartened the surviving defenders at Sidi Rezegh – until the dug-in 88mm guns began to bark, and one after another of the approaching tanks flashed into flame.

Meanwhile, the 5th South African Brigade, which had moved up the day before but which had been kept clear of the armoured battle, was ordered to capture the southern part of the escarpment where German troops and artillery were dug in, particularly around a high spot, Point 178. The attack, launched with great gallantry at about 15.00, was repulsed with heavy loss, the South Africans being forced to withdraw two miles, where they encountered what was left of 22nd Armoured Brigade.

The whole desert landscape, once more under grey skies and swept by a biting wind, was an inferno of bursting shells, drifting clouds of sand kicked up by explosions, and the smoke from burning tanks and vehicles. This terrible fog of war so obscured the battlefield that when the 4th Armoured Brigade arrived at a point five miles to the east, it could not distinguish between friend and foe and was unable to help.

Neither could the ground-attack squadrons of the Desert Air Force. Although its bomber squadrons attacked targets in the rear areas, battlefield support was out of the question, so great was the chaos.

Nightfall saw the airfield at Sidi Rezegh firmly in German hands. Meanwhile, 15th *Panzer* Division, which had been lying to the east, had been ordered to carry out a wide encircling movement to join in the battle from the south-west. This plan was changed when, in response to a call for assistance from 21st *Panzer*, it turned and headed straight for the battlefield.

As its tanks forged ahead in the desert darkness, they ran into the luckless 4th Armoured Brigade, which was preparing to go into laager for the night. The Germans were the first to recover from the surprise and a furious night action ensued, the battle lit by headlights, flares, blazing tanks and gunfire. The Germans captured fifty armoured fighting vehicles, Brigade Headquarters and many prisoners. It would be more than twenty-four hours before the 4th Armoured Brigade could put up even a token show of strength.

The next day, Sunday, 23 November, was the day on which the Germans remembered the fallen of the Great War. It was called *Totensonntag*, the Sunday of the Dead, and it cast an ominous shadow over what was to come. Even the weather was forbidding; the sky was once again heavily overcast, the wind icy. There was also a heavy mist.

Through it, like phantoms, came the tanks of 15th

Panzer, now under orders to join up with the Italian *Ariete* Division. Unexpectedly, they came upon the Support Group and transport of 5th South African Brigade, and when a regiment of 21st *Panzer* arrived to join the battle, the fate of the South Africans was sealed. All that day they fought to the death, but by nightfall they had lost two-thirds of their men and all their equipment. The remnants of the brigade withdrew southwards, having ceased to exist as an effective fighting force. Meanwhile, XIII Corps had been making good progress on the eastern flank. The New Zealand Division, besides taking Sollum barracks and part of the Sidi Rezegh escarpment, was now only six miles from the airfield.

During the morning of 24 November, General Crüwell, out of contact with Rommel and acting on his own initiative, decided to force a showdown with the remaining British armour at Sidi Rezegh. There was little finesse behind his plan. By early afternoon he had concentrated the *Ariete* Division and two *Panzer* regiments in line abreast near Bir el Gubi, and at 15.00 hours the whole formation, with two regiments of motorised infantry in close support, began moving north through a thin drizzle towards the dug-in German infantry and artillery on the escarpment at Sidi Rezegh.

Between the German armour and the escarpment lay the tanks and artillery of the 7th Armoured Division, which opened up an intense fire as the *Panzers* rolled towards them in what seemed like a suicidal cavalry charge.

The Germans use the expression *abgeschossen* – shot down – to describe the destruction of an enemy tank.

They use exactly the same word for the destruction of an enemy aircraft. The British, on the other hand, say that a stricken tank is 'brewed up', which in many ways is a more apt description, although it does not convey the horror of the event.

A shell that pierces the armour plate of a tank and explodes inside ignites everything, sending tongues of flame curling out of every orifice. Shells and machine-gun bullets begin to explode, adding to the inferno, so that the convulsing, melting body of the tank becomes the centre of a fierce pyrotechnic display. Its crew will be torn asunder, burnt to cinders. Some may escape, only to be cut down by shards of flying metal, exploding ammunition or enemy small arms fire. Multiply this scenario by two hundred, and you will have some small inkling of the hell that was Sidi Rezegh, on that Sunday of the Dead.

By 18.00 hours, Crüwell's forces had joined up with Rommel. The *Panzers* had suffered fearsome losses in their wild charge across the desert, but the crude brute-force tactics had resulted in the annihilation of the British 7th Armoured Division and most of the 1st South African Division.

Rommel now formed an audacious plan. The next morning, he would hurl his two *Panzer* divisions eastward along the Trigh el Abd to the frontier wire, falling upon and destroying the enemy support echelons that were reported to be massing there. The British forces already inside Libya would be completely cut off; he could turn upon them and hack them to pieces at his leisure. Within a week, the Eighth Army would be no more.

Fifteen

Monday, 25 November 1941. The Battlefield

K alinski looked down aghast from the cockpit of his Hurricane. For the last few minutes he had seen nothing but Axis tanks and transport, rolling eastward in the direction of the Egyptian frontier. Only now, as he carried out the first thorough reconnaissance of the battle area for several days, did he begin to appreciate the scale of the disaster that had overwhelmed the armoured spearhead of XXX Corps.

Dense columns of smoke rose from the desert, mingling with the cloud that hung overhead in an unbroken layer. The desert floor was strewn with the smouldering remains of tanks, most of them British.

After a few more minutes, Kalinski had seen enough. He flew back to Landing Ground 125 and reported to Armstrong. The latter's face was grim as he briefed the pilots.

"Rommel has got to be stopped," he told them. "According to Flight Lieutenant Kalinski's report his leading echelons are now at Gabr Saleh, about halfway between Sidi Rezegh and the wire. We've got to hit them hard, and keep on hitting them until the cloud cover breaks and the Desert Air Force's medium bomber squadrons can operate effectively. One thing is in our favour," he added. "From what we've just heard, anything that's moving is pretty certain to be German or Italian. That's what has been holding us back until now, the danger of hitting our own people. But now we can really get at 'em."

Thirty minutes later the first of the three squadrons at LG 125, a South African Kittyhawk unit, began taking off. It was followed soon afterwards by the second Kittyhawk squadron, this one manned by Australians. Each Kittyhawk carried a pair of 250-pound bombs on racks under its wings.

The Hurricanes were the last to take off. Armstrong and Baird walked out to their aircraft together. Armstrong was still worried about his friend, who seemed distant and withdrawn. If I'd had any sense, he told himself, I'd have taken Dickie off flying. But he knew that he needed Baird's expertise and leadership qualities; when this show was over, he'd do something about it.

Today's operation was going to be no picnic, but as far as Armstrong's ground-attack squadrons were concerned Rommel's sudden dash for the frontier had produced one unexpected advantage: his forces were now some thirty miles closer to LG 125 than had been the case a couple of days earlier. That meant, in terms of the round trip, that sixty miles were now chopped off the distance the attacking aircraft had to fly – a crucial factor for pilots operating close to the limits of their aircrafts' combat radius. This was particularly true of the Kittyhawks, carrying the extra burden of their bomb load.

The attackers located the enemy force without difficulty; its dust cloud could be seen for miles. The Kittyhawks fanned out into line abreast and swept down on the enemy column just as Armstrong's Hurricanes arrived on the scene. The fighter-bomber pilots had learned in training that attacking diagonally across an enemy column usually produced good results; there was a better chance of their bombs hitting something, or at least of scoring a disabling near miss, than was the case if they attacked along the line of transport.

Flashes of flame and mushrooms of smoke told that at least some of the bombs were on target. The enemy column began to scatter, its cohesion temporarily broken. Recovering from their initial surprise, the enemy began opening fire on the speeding Kittyhawks, scattered lines of tracer becoming thicker until the sky above the desert was dense with flying metal.

After their bombing run, the Kittyhawk pilots made several strafing passes, their six heavy-calibre Browning 0.5-inch lethal against anything other than a tank. Two of the aircraft were shot down, crashing to earth in a flare of exploding fuel tanks. The rest reformed and headed back to their base, shepherded by the Hurricanes, whose pilots, on Armstrong's orders, had also used up their ammunition on some enemy trucks, once it had become apparent that the *Luftwaffe* was not going to make an appearance.

Back at the airfield, ground crews rapidly turned round the aircraft, rearming and refuelling them in readiness for a second sortie while the pilots gratefully sipped mugs of hot, sweet tea. There was no time to dwell on those who had not returned; each man was aware that he might have to fly three or four sorties in the course of the day, and self-preservation was the keyword.

Armstrong had made up his mind about one thing. He went over the Baird, who was sitting on a rock apart from the others, staring moodily into his mug of tea.

"Dickie, I'm taking you off flying," Armstrong said firmly, without any preamble.

Baird looked up at him. There was a curious expression on his face, a mixture of relief and something indefinable, a hint, perhaps, of the way people sometimes look when they feel they have let someone down.

"I'm quite all right, Ken, really I am," Baird said, getting up slowly and facing his commanding officer.

"No, you're not," Armstrong told him abruptly. "I was following you down when you were strafing that flak truck. You were flying straight down the line of tracer, mesmerised, and you'd have flown straight into the bloody truck if I hadn't yelled at you to pull out. You're off flying until further notice, and that's an order."

Armstrong turned on his heel and strode off towards his Hurricane. Baird sat down heavily on his rock and stared at his friend's retreating back. He lit a cigarette, and noticed with some surprise that his hands were no longer shaking.

Armstrong quietly told Eamonn O'Day to take over command of 'B' Flight, and also informed Kalinski of his decision. The Pole nodded, casting a covertly sympathetic glance towards where Baird still sat moodily on his rock. "It could happen to any of us," he said.

"Heaven knows, Dickie has seen more than his fair share of action."

There was no replacement pilot available to fly Baird's Hurricane, but that couldn't be helped, Armstrong thought, as he led his slightly depleted formation back towards the battle front. As he flew on, he noticed that the overcast was starting to break up, which meant that the Desert Air Force would soon be able to throw all its resources into the battle.

What Armstrong did not know was that the Desert Air Force was in some disarray following the hurried withdrawal of a couple of Blenheim squadrons which had moved up to forward airstrips in the wake of XXX Corps' advance. So rapid had been Rommel's dash eastwards that General Cunningham, the Eighth Army commander, had only just escaped by the skin of his teeth in a Blenheim as the *Panzers* roared towards the rough airstrip at Gabr Saleh. But the *Luftwaffe* and the Italian Air Force were in no better shape; they, too, had been forced to make a hurried exit from Gambut and other bases at the start of the British offensive. It was all a question of which side sorted itself out first.

By midday on 25 November, however, the Germans had reorganised themselves sufficiently to carry out defensive patrols over Rommel's forward echelons, and Eduard Neumann's JG 27 was at the forefront, as usual. Now, in response to an urgent request for air cover from the *Afrika Korps*, Hans-Joachim Marseille was leading eight Messerschmitts in a wide sweep over the area between Sidi Omar and Gabr Saleh when he sighted the Kittyhawks coming in for their second attack of the day.

Marseille brought his pilots round in a broad turn, placing them astern of the Kittyhawks, then took them down in a screaming dive as the fighter-bombers were making their run. It was the South African squadron that bore the brunt of the attack; the pilots, intent on their targets, failed to see the approaching danger until it was too late, and within seconds three of them were going down in flames.

Under cover of the ensuing dogfight the Australian pilots attacked in their turn, then climbed to join the battle just as Armstrong's Hurricanes appeared on the scene. Marseille ordered his pilots to concentrate on the latter, realising that they presented a greater danger than the more cumbersome Kittyhawks.

With aircraft scattered all over the sky, Marseille decided to climb a few thousand feet into the clearing sky and assess the situation. With his faithful wingman sticking to him like glue, he circled like a hawk, seeking his prey. Almost immediately below him a Messerschmitt flashed into view, twisting and turning as it tried to shake off the Hurricane that was pursuing it.

Still followed by Rainer Pottger, Marseille dived hard after the pair, working his way into a position from which he could be certain of a kill. He was almost ready to open fire when a cry of alarm came over the radio from Pottger, who had suddenly come under attack by a lone Kittyhawk.

"Deal with him, Rainer," Marseille said calmly, and continued to close in on the Hurricane. The Me 109 in front of the British fighter suddenly began to smoke; an instant later it turned over on its back, the cockpit canopy flew off, and the dark shape of the pilot emerged, arms and legs spreadeagled.

Marseille felt a cold anger. He was closing fast on the Hurricane, his finger poised on the gun trigger. Just a second or two more, Jochen, he breathed to himself. The first burst will kill him.

Ahead of him, Armstrong was awaiting his moment, too. When a sixth sense told him that the German was about to open fire, he suddenly closed the throttle and at the same moment pulled the Hurricane into a high-g barrel roll. The theory behind the manoeuvre was that the attacking aircraft's higher speed would take it through the centre of the roll, allowing the defender to complete the manoeuvre and increase speed to dive after his opponent.

"Not this time, my friend!" Marseille yelled out loud in exaltation, realising that the British pilot had started the manoeuvre just a little too soon. Quickly, the German pulled up into a steep climb, then winged over and arrowed down towards Armstrong's aircraft as it hung halfway round the roll, its energy dissipated.

A shout of triumph over the radio had already told Marseille that Pottger had disposed of the Kittyhawk. His wingman would soon rejoin him and fall into his accustomed position, guarding the leader's tail.

The Hurricane was upside down, its pale blue belly naked and exposed. Goodbye, my friend, Marseille thought.

At that instant, his instrument panel exploded in front of his eyes and choking coolant fumes invaded the cockpit. Unable to see, he flung the Messerschmitt on its wingtip and pulled it round in a tight turn. He pulled a toggle and the cockpit hood whirled away, admitting a blast of freezing air into the cockpit. The fumes cleared and he was able to see again. Wildly, he looked around. There was no sign of whatever had attacked him. In fact, there was no sign of any other aircraft.

"Rainer, where the devil are you?" he called.

"I have you in sight, sir," his wingman replied. "You are trailing a thin stream of smoke. Are you all right?"

"I'll make it, Rainer. I'll make it. My compass is shot, though. You'll have to steer me home."

The two Messerschmitts headed west. Marseille's engine was running roughly, but it would get him to an airstrip. He vowed, as he flew along, that he would never again start an attack with his tail unguarded.

His would-be victim was thinking much the same thoughts as he headed south for the landing ground. He had almost been caught with his pants down, and only a stroke of luck and the timely intervention of another fighter had saved his bacon.

A few miles south of the battlefield, another Hurricane dropped into place off his starboard wingtip. Its pilot was looking at him, only his eyes visible above his oxygen mask. A voice with a very familiar Scots accent crackled over the R/T.

"It's a good job I never take any notice of you," Baird said.

Hans-Joachim Marseille was not the only one to suffer a trauma that day. Shortly before midnight, a rubber dinghy came drifting in towards the African coast, its occupant cold, wet and utterly miserable. It had not been a good day for *Capitano* Umberto Ricci, whose squadron was now based at Derna. Shortly after dawn he had been dispatched to make a shipping reconnaissance of the Channel between Libya and Crete, a task that fell routinely to the Italian single-engined fighter pilots, and one they disliked intensely.

Ricci had not found any ships of importance. Nor had he seen the flock of seagulls until it was too late, and the luckless birds were impacting on his aircraft with the force of anti-aircraft shells, shattering its propeller. So, for hours on end, Ricci had drifted in his dinghy, his only comfort being that the coast was growing steadily larger with the passage of time.

By midnight he could actually smell the shore, its scent borne on a light breeze, and he began to paddle furiously towards it. He had no idea where he was, and if the area was uninhabited, with no source of water, his life would still be in danger.

When he saw the aircraft moored at the entrance to a small inlet, and recognized it for what it was, his joy therefore knew no bounds. He would be safe now. He called out, and a voice answered him in what sounded like German.

A few minutes later, almost babbling his gratitude, Ricci was being pulled into the interior of the floatplane. He stood upright, facing a shadowy figure, and gasped as something hard jabbed into his midriff.

"Welcome aboard," Erik Hansen said.

Epilogue

The British offensive in Libya almost foundered on the wreckage of Sidi Rezegh; almost, but not quite. For three days, while the men of the Tobruk garrison clung desperately to the ground they had gained in the salient, the Allied commanders fought hard to regroup their scattered, dislocated forces, to check Rommel's dash for the frontier and push the offensive forward once more.

During those three days, the men of the Desert Air Force flew continually, striking the enemy's armoured columns wherever they were to be found. It was a difficult, thankless task, for amid all the confusion, chaos and panic it was often hard to distinguish friend from foe, and communications with Eighth Army HQ were badly disrupted. The Germans swept on, still menacing the forward airstrips, and pilots were ordered to sleep under the wings of their aircraft in case their bases were suddenly attacked.

At one landing ground, just to the east of Fort Maddalena and inside Egyptian territory, over 175 fighters and bombers stood wingtip to wingtip. A German *Panzer* group passed less than ten miles to the north and failed to see the airfield in the darkness. Had they done so, they could easily have wiped out most of the Desert Air Force's effective fighter strength.

In the afternoon of 26 November, the New Zealand Division made contact with elements of the Tobruk garrison at El Duda, and a corridor to the port was open for the first time in seven months. The battle, however, was far from over. On the following day Rommel, strongly opposed on the ground, abandoned his thrust into Egypt and brought his *Panzers* racing back across the desert to Tobruk. By the end of the month they had once again succeeded in capturing Sidi Rezegh and closing the corridor.

The Desert Air Force continued to harry the enemy columns mercilessly. For Armstrong and his pilots, as for all the others, the first week of December was a confusion of roaring engines, of brief periods of exhausted sleep, and of sudden, blinding dust-storms. And gradually, as the days passed, Rommel's forces were compelled to yield ground.

On 5 December, Kalinski, carrying out a routine reconnaissance, reported large concentrations of enemy transport streaming westwards past Tobruk. The Hurricanes, now converted into fighter-bombers with 250-pound bombs mounted on wing racks, joined the Kittyhawks in meting out severe punishment, leaving an estimated thirty vehicles in flames.

Two days later, the Tobruk corridor was once more open, and now Rommel's forces were clearly in full withdrawal towards Gazala.

On that day – a day which, in the words of United States President Franklin D. Roosevelt, would live in infamy – the bombers of Imperial Japan swept down on the American naval base at Pearl Harbor, Hawaii.

It was now, truly, a global war.